SAGA OF THE SIX WORLDS

RITE OF BROTHERHOOD

CHERITH BALDRY

Chariot Books™
A Division of Cook Communications

Chariot Books™ is an imprint of David C. Cook Publishing Co.
David C. Cook Publishing Co., Elgin, Illinois 60120
David C. Cook Publishing Co., Weston, Ontario
Nova Distribution Ltd., Eastbourne, England

RITE OF BROTHERHOOD
© 1990, 1994 by Cherith Baldry

Designed by Foster Design
Cover illustration by David Moses
First Printing, Revised Edition, 1994

Printed in the United States of America
98 97 96 95 94 5 4 3 2 1

Library of Congress Cataloging-in-Publication Data
Baldry, Cherith.
[Hostage of the sea]
p.   cm.
Previously published as: Hostage of the sea.
"Saga of the six worlds"—Cover.
Summary: Fifteen-year-old Aurion, being held hostage by a belligerent island king who is
planning the conquest of their entire ocean planet, hopes to prevent war by introducing
his enemies to the one true God.
ISBN 0-7814-0094-5
[1. Science fiction.   2. Christian life—Fiction.] I. Title.
PZ7.B18175Ri   1994
[Fic]—dc20   94-17037
                                                                        CIP
                                                                         AC

First published in 1990 as *Hostage of the Sea* by Kingsway Publications Ltd., Eastbourne,
England

British ISBN 0-86065-730-2

Pronunciation of Some
Names on Ocean

Arax   Ar'ax ("a" as in "cat")

Aurion   Ow'rion ("i" as in "fit")

Hana   Hah'na (the first "a" as in "bar")

Hithiel   Hith'iel

Kerraven   Kerr'aven ("a" as in "cat")

Largh   "gh" pronounced like "ch" in Scottish
                    "Loch"

Meriu   Mer'ioo ("i" as in "fit")

To William

The Six Worlds

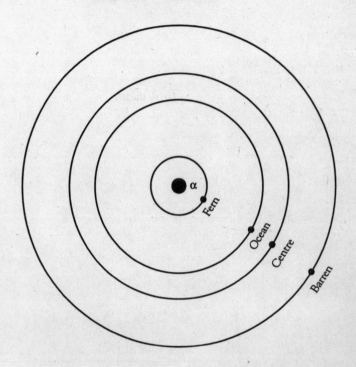

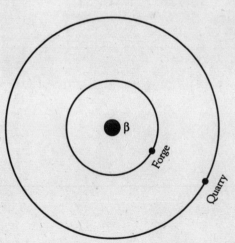

The Six Worlds and their two suns, Alpha and Beta, form a binary system. Beta takes several thousand years to make one circuit of Alpha.

This plan is not to scale.

I always revered my father as a great king. In fact, as king of the Two Islands, he was the ruler of half a dozen villages—a thousand people, more or less. Now it seems an absurdity, but in those days the islands were my world. My father was all-powerful, wise, just, and merciful. And to me he was kind and patient. Even now when I have traveled farther and seen more than he ever did, I can still appreciate his insight and his strength. He was truly a great king.

When I was a child I wandered freely over the islands, and there was no home where I was not welcome. I learned to swim and sail a boat, to read and write, and to know the true God who made all worlds. From my father I learned the craft of healing. So it never seemed strange to me that a king should sit by the bed of a dying fisherman.

On the whole I was contented. I heard, of course, of other island kingdoms—greater kingdoms than ours, perhaps, but none, I thought, so well governed. And I heard other even more wonderful stories about ships that could fly through the sky and carry men from world to world scattered through the heavens like the islands of Ocean scattered over the sea. At first I doubted these until my father assured me they were true. But they never meant very much to me. Until I was fifteen years old, my life was mapped out for me, secure in the love of my people and a task that I could do. Until the day the ship came.

I had been out all day sailing to West Island, and the sun was setting behind me as I tacked across the straits. Ahead there was still light in the sky, and East Island was all golden like an enchanted land in a tale. I had seen it like this more times than I could count, but now from the shoulder of the hill that hid my home village and my father's house, a smudge of smoke rose into the sky. I could not see what was burning, but I knew something was wrong.

I tightened my sail, impatient to be home but afraid of what I might find. As I brought the boat around the point to the bay, I could see that the houses in the village were blazing. Anchored just offshore I saw the ship. I had never seen a warship before but I knew what it was—long and rakish, painted like a great sea monster, and with armed men at watch on the deck.

As I drew closer I could hear shouting and screaming from the cluster of white houses, half-shrouded now in smoke, and see here and there running or struggling figures, and the flash of swords. My home, higher up the hill, seemed still quiet and untouched. I beached the boat and was out and crossing the strip of sand before I let myself feel fear. I was unarmed—we are not fighters in the Two Islands—without even a hunting knife. I was not sure what I could do. But I knew that a king, or a king's son, has no choice but to stand with his people.

At the corner of the first house I collided with one of the warriors who was dragging along a woman with a small child. The child was screaming and the woman struggling to resist, but she was helpless. I grabbed the warrior's sword arm and bore down on it. He was surprised, and for a few seconds I held him.

"My lord!" the woman cried. "My lord, don't—"

"Run!" I gasped at her. With a sob she tore herself free, scooped up the child, and was gone. The man thrust at me savagely, and I fell back to the ground. His sword was at my throat.

It seemed an eternity that I lay there, keeping my eyes on his, but still aware of the death that hovered a breath away. He was tall and fair, his tunic and his helmet plume were scarlet, and the sun dazzled on his armor. I could not read his face, or what he meant to do to me. Then he stepped back and ordered me to get up.

"She called you my lord," he reflected. "Who are you, lad?"

I stood erect.

Chapter 1

"My name is Aurion. The king is my father."

He smiled at that slowly. He was beginning to speak again when he was interrupted by a horn call from somewhere behind us, toward the center of the village. With the sword he gestured to me sharply, and I walked before him, the point of his weapon pricking my back in the direction of the call.

The houses of the village were built around an open space, and here the raiders were assembling. In the drifting smoke that caught at my throat and eyes, I could see that they were forming into ranks. Suddenly I understood. They had finished with the village. Now they were moving on farther up the hill toward my father's house.

My captor thrust me forward toward the man who was clearly their leader. But before he could speak there was another disturbance. From the path that led up the hill, my father appeared at the head of a small group of men. They were armed, but even inexperienced as I was, I could see they were hopelessly outmatched.

Then my father saw me, and stopped dead.

"Aurion!"

The leader stepped forward and confronted him. "You lead this rabble?"

"I am their king."

"And this?" He nodded at me.

"My son."

His sword rose only a little way toward me; he never took his eyes off my father.

"Tell your men to put down their weapons."

"No!" I cried.

No one took any notice of me. My father stood calmly, assessing the situation, and then nodded. There was a clatter as the men behind him dropped or put away their weapons. He sheathed his own sword. His mouth was hard, but his voice was quiet as he spoke.

"Who are you? What do you want?"

Their leader bowed his head, but from the look on his face there was mockery in the gesture of respect.

"I come with greetings from Largh, king of Tar-Askar, my lord and your kinsman. He sends you his regrets that he has so far neglected the Two Islands and bids me negotiate the terms of your alliance with him."

"And does Largh negotiate at the point of a sword?"

"My lord wishes to make the situation perfectly clear." He raised his voice a little. "I sailed from Tar-Askar with one ship. At need my lord could send out a hundred. You would do well to consider his terms very carefully."

"And they are?"

In the midst of fire and ruin my father still refused to show fear.

"Perhaps we could discuss that in more suitable place?"

"Very well. Will you and your men accept the hospitality of my house?"

The leader nodded and rapped out an order to his men. My father held out a hand to me.

"Aurion."

I went to him. No one tried to stop me. My father rested his hand on my shoulder as he gave instructions to his own men to begin repairs in the village. Then he motioned to me to precede him up the path. Behind us, the armed warriors of Tar-Askar closed in and followed.

2

The courtyard of my father's house was empty, and the carved wooden doors stood wide open. It seemed as if not one of the household remained. The Tar-Askan leader gave another order to his men, and they drew up before the doors in disciplined silence. They might have seemed splendid with their plumes and weapons, their armor flashing gold in the last rays of the sun. Yet I was afraid.

Then my father—courteously, as if inviting a guest—motioned to the leader to enter. I was not sure what to do. I started to follow, but my father turned to me with a half-smile and said, "You look a mess, Aurion. Go and have a bath and change. I'll see you at supper."

Naturally I obeyed him. So I never knew what was said at that first meeting between my father and the leader of the Tar-Askans.

Supper, at the usual hour, was ceremonial—a meal such as I had attended only a few times, for we had few important guests in the Two Islands. Somehow my father had reassembled the household to provide well-cooked food, the best wine, and a musician. He spoke to the Tar-Askan as if he were the ambassador of an equal and friendly power. Seated beside him at the high table in the great hall, I tried to imitate him, but all through the meal I could not forget the truth, or stop wondering what was going to happen to us now.

At last it was over. My father said goodnight to the Tar-Askan, sending a servant to conduct him to his lodging. Then he drew me aside into his own private room. With a sigh that showed how weary he was, he poured himself a last cup of wine and sank down into a chair by the unkindled fire.

I brought a stool and sat at his feet. For all the questions I had to ask, I had been taught how to behave, and I would never have dreamed of asking them before he spoke to me. At last he sighed once again.

"These men who have come today . . ."

"Yes, Father?"

"You heard what they said. They are from Tar-Askar, the kingdom to the south."

I nodded. I had heard of it before, of its splendors and its power—and its cruelty.

"They call themselves an embassy." He smiled grimly. "After all, it is an effective style of diplomacy. We know now that we have no hope of resisting them."

He was silent for a moment and then went on. "The king of Tar-Askar is my cousin."

I was startled; I had not known.

"Or perhaps a more remote kinship, but he styles himself cousin." His hand moved as if he brushed away an insect. "Though that has little to do with the matter. His ambassador requests—no, demands—that we acknowledge his master as our overlord. He requires tribute from us. And he requires a hostage."

For the first time he touched me, a hand lightly on my shoulder.

"Aurion, this is hard for me to say, but there is no alternative. You must go to Tar-Askar."

I sat very still. I remember the lamplight flooding golden over the paved floor. Outside a night bird was calling. I looked at my clasped hands and the woven border of my linen tunic. Only one answer was possible.

"Of course, Father, if you wish it."

"I do not wish it!" There was suppressed anger in his voice. I had scarcely ever heard him angry.

"I do not wish it, but I must command it. Perhaps if you had not drawn attention to yourself this afternoon. . . ." He smiled again, more warmly this time, and I could see he was pleased with me.

"You did well, Aurion. And I could not have hidden that I have a son. At least they know now that he has spirit."

His smile faded.

"Aurion, you saw the men outside. There are more on board the ship. That one ship could destroy the Islands. They would kill and burn and loot. We're not fighting men, Aurion. We have always lived for peace. And so I must give in to what my cousin asks. You must go."

I sat with bowed head. I knew he was right. I did not wish to see the villages in flames and our people dead, or terrified and enslaved. But something in me was crying out in protest and fear when I thought of what lay ahead.

When I could, I turned to him again and asked, "How long must I stay there, Father?"

He shook his head. "I do not know."

"But then . . ." It was hard to find the words for what I needed to say. "Father, I have so much to learn here. You have said so yourself—that I must be ready for the day I take your place—"

He raised a hand to stop me.

"I'm sorry, Aurion. But such things are not in our hands any longer. It will be my cousin who decides who shall rule in the Two Islands."

Then I knew I was to lose my inheritance as well as my home.

Out of fear and love I had never spoken rebelliously to my father, but now the words came welling up in me—bitter, wild reproaches for everything he was casting aside. Somehow I controlled my tongue and said nothing. When I looked up at him again and met his eyes, I saw that he understood. And I understood, too, that neither of us had any choice because whatever the Tar-Askans did to us, he was still a king, and I his son. And we must take the only way that would save our people.

He was silent again, for a long time, and when he finally spoke, he sounded less sure of himself.

"In Tar-Askar," he told me, "they do not worship the true God."

His words only increased my fears. Was I to lose that as well as everything else?

"They worship, I believe, a sea god they call Askar. And the people are what their god makes them—proud, cruel, and always seeking power. You know Aurion, this expedition to the Two Islands isn't their only conquest. Their ambassador made that clear. They're extending themselves over this whole section of Ocean. If they could, they would make themselves masters of all the world."

I shivered.

"And if that is what they want, very soon they must come into conflict with Kerraven."

I listened more attentively and forgot, in part, my own problems. Kerraven was our nearest neighbor to the northwest— a large kingdom, and friendly to us. We traded with them regularly, and though I had never been there, I felt I knew it quite well.

"In Kerraven they worship the true God," my father went on. "They do not want war. But war will be forced on them if Tar-Askar goes on pushing outward. And then little kingdoms like the Two Islands won't escape. We could see the whole of our world go up in flames."

He bent over me, put a hand on my head, and looked down at me attentively. I tried to meet his eyes and conceal my fear and uncertainty.

"There seems no way to avert this war," he said. "Two great kingdoms must meet and clash, except that you now are going to Tar-Askar. Aurion, I believe that God works through small events and unlikely people. Perhaps He is sending you there to show them a God of peace. Perhaps you can avert this war with Kerraven."

Now I was terrified. I wanted to cry out to him, "I'm not like that, I'm not strong enough," but I could say nothing of that. I was his son. He believed in me. He said I had done well in the raid. At last, under his eyes, I asked uncertainly, "What must I do?"

"Not bring the whole nation to God all in a moment," he

said, smiling. "My kinsman is probably set in his ways and will not take kindly to change. But he has a son—I can't remember his name—about your age. He might listen to you. Or there may be others—enough to see that war is not the only way of life."

He gripped my shoulders and I felt a sudden strength, though I knew I would feel very different when I was alone in Tar-Askar without him.

"If Tar-Askar goes to war with Kerraven no one will truly win. There will only be destruction. Aurion, believe me, I know what I'm asking of you. But no one else is in your position. You must do what you can to stop this war."

He paused and added more quietly, "The king's son—no, I don't remember his name."

3

His name was Arax. I saw him for the first time standing beside his father's throne in the great hall of the palace in Tar-Askar. It was a fortnight since I had said good-bye to my father. I will pass over the pain of that parting; I was sure I would never see him again. I had never traveled so far before, and by the time I knelt at the feet of Largh of Tar-Askar, I was tired, disheveled, and more convinced than ever that I could do nothing to carry out my father's task.

I handed him the letter my father had written to him, and he kept me there, kneeling at his feet, while he read it. I watched him. He was tall and broad with a hawk's face and gray hair that had once been golden. I had only to look at his son standing beside him to see how splendid he must have been as a young man.

The letter read, he handed it to his son and turned his scrutiny on to me.

"You are Aurion?"

"Yes, my lord."

"You understand why you are here?"

"Yes, my lord."

He looked approving, and settled himself more easily in the gilded seat.

"I do not expect trouble from your father, in which case you need expect no trouble here. You will train with the other young men of the court and live as they do. What you make of your life here will be up to you." He gave me a humorless smile.

"I don't bid you welcome. I know well enough what your thoughts of me must be. But you'll find I can reward loyalty and diligence."

He stopped as if he expected me to say something, but I had no idea what, and so kept silent. After a pause he went on.

"There is one more thing. In the Two Islands, you worship some strange god—a god who died?"

Perhaps this was my first opportunity to speak eloquently before the whole court of the true nature of our God. At that moment I could just as easily have flown.

"Yes, my lord."

"Here we worship Askar, God of the Sea." He bent forward. "Your father asks me that you may have leave to follow your own customs. This I grant, but with discretion—you understand?"

"Yes, my lord. Thank you."

His permission was more than I had expected, though it did not offer much hope for what I must do. Yet I felt only relief to have the matter settled for the time being, and greater relief still when Largh ordered me to rise and waved me to a place among the courtiers who thronged the sides of the hall. I was glad not to be the focus of attention while the king dealt with other matters, and for the first time I was able to look around me.

The hall was much larger than the one in my father's house. Sunlight poured through windows set high in the walls. The walls themselves were painted with bright pictures, but no brighter than the robes of the courtiers. I was bewildered by the shifting mass of color. The air was hot and thick with perfume, and I wondered how much longer the audience would continue. I desperately wanted to get out of there, to be alone, but instead I knew I would have to face this new place, new companions, a whole new life. Then there was a touch on my arm.

"Follow me, my lord."

It was a servant who had spoken to me. I followed him as he threaded a way through the press of courtiers and out through a side door that led to a covered passageway. At the end of the passage I could see another door standing open, and through it a dazzle of white and blue that resolved itself into a terrace overlooking the sea. As I stepped outside, the servant withdrew, closing the door behind me.

"Hello, little cousin."

I turned and saw him. He had stood beside Largh in the hall, and I had already guessed he was the king's son. Now he sat on the low wall of the terrace with one foot on the ground, the other swinging slowly. He was tall and golden-haired with sea-green eyes that were fixed on me narrowly. Neither the eyes, nor the half smile, nor the tone of his voice was wholly friendly. I tried to sound firm.

"Cousin, my lord?"

The respectful title slipped out naturally. His smile broadened a little.

"I am Arax, the king's son. Our fathers are cousins, so they tell me." He patted the wall at his side. "Come and sit here."

I sat hesitantly. I had the sense of approaching something dangerous, like a leopard. He had the cat's grace and unpredictability. Already it was occurring to me that this was the person who was supposed to listen to me and be influenced against the war. The idea seemed ridiculous.

"And how do you like Tar-Askar, little cousin?"

"I . . . don't know."

"You will like it when you see it. Perhaps I shall show it to you. Perhaps . . . though after all," he added, "you must stay whether you like it or not. For myself, I should have been glad to leave that barren rock you came from. This is the greatest kingdom on all Ocean."

There seemed nothing I could say to that, and he seemed not to expect a reply.

"So you are to train with us," he went on. "Do you know what we train for?"

"No, my lord."

"For war." He laughed complacently. "Don't think we really want your Two Islands," he told me. "You don't matter. But you were in the way. We have greater things to do."

He laughed again. "Those fools in Kerraven don't know what lies ahead."

He looked me over once more.

"What did they say your name was?"

"Aurion, my lord."

"Aurion. Well, Aurion, little cousin, you don't look like a warrior. But perhaps your appearance doesn't do you justice. Are you any good with a sword?"

I shook my head.

"Bow, then? Spear?"

"No, my lord."

The sea-green eyes were fixed on me now, genuinely shocked. "Then what do you do?"

"We live a . . . a different life in the Two Islands."

He drew his head back. Now, I thought, the claws will unsheathe. But he said, almost indifferently, "That is why one Tar-Askan ship could defeat you. It's why you're here now."

It was true. And for a moment I almost wished that we were warriors too, and could have driven the Tar-Askans back into the sea. Then I would never have left my home . . . but it was no use. I knew that way was not for me. Somehow I had to make Arax understand it too.

"My lord, if you would listen. . . . It's wrong to make war on us, or on Kerraven—"

As I spoke I reached out toward him, and it was as if my movement had unleashed him. With frightening swiftness he was on me. He grasped my shoulders and thrust me back over the low wall so that his grip was all that kept me from falling. I could not restrain a gasp of terror.

"Frightened, little cousin?" he asked.

I tried to twist my head to see how far I had to fall. Earlier I had been looking at him, and I did not know if below me there was another terrace, or rocks, or the sea. He wore a coiled bronze snake around his forearm, and the jeweled eyes flashed at me as I struggled.

"Don't do that," he warned. "I might have to let go."

I was still, then rigid, looking up at him.

"You know why you're there, don't you?" he asked. "Because I'm stronger than you, and faster, and I moved first. But you might be able to persuade me to let you up again. Why don't you try?"

I was silent. Whatever he did to me, whatever he said, I was not going to plead for my life. Though already in imagination I could trace the plunging fall, the shock of impact on sharp rocks below. Seconds dragged by.

"Go on—ask."

His face, inches from mine, was fierce now—the lazy smile gone. I wanted to close my eyes and shut it out, but I made myself go on looking at him. Then suddenly he hauled me upward and released me on my knees. Clinging to the wall, I looked down. Not far below was another terrace, brilliant with banks of flowers. I might have been hurt in a fall, but not killed. When I looked up again Arax was gone, and I heard his voice at a distance calling for the servant who came to take me to my room.

The layout of the palace bewildered me that first day. It was built around a series of courtyards and terraces made beautiful with flowers and falling water, and shaded by a long row of columns. My room opened off one of these. It was much larger than my own room at home and much more elaborately furnished. The walls were painted like those in the great hall. The furniture was of pale, polished wood, richly carved. And there were hangings of embroidered linen and silk. I was being lodged, I supposed, like a king's son, yet I yearned for the simple austerity of my father's house.

The possessions I had brought with me—not very many—were already in the room when I arrived. The servant left me to unpack after offering to do it for me.

"The evening meal is in an hour, my lord," he informed me. "I shall come back to show you where to go." He ran a critical eye over me. "You should change, my lord."

"Could I have a bath?"

"Of course, my lord. I will see to it."

When he had gone, I undid my bundles and found places for everything. I found I was dragging out the task, for it seemed a link with the home I had lost. Clothes—which I guessed were not going to be fine enough for Tar-Askar—a little money, which we scarcely used in the Two Islands, and a few personal treasures like an engraved hunting knife in a worked leather sheath. The greatest treasure of all I was wearing: a cross, carved from whalebone, that had come from Kerraven. It was my father's parting gift.

"It's the sign of our Lord," he said as he passed the chain over my head. "He may seem very remote in Tar-Askar. But He is with you—as close to you as this."

I had not quite finished when the servant returned. He took me to the bathhouse where, fortunately, there was not enough time for the ceremony that he would have preferred. Then he took me to the dining hall for the evening meal. I was afraid of encountering Arax again, but he was seated on the high table beside his father, whereas I was shown to a place in the body of the hall, next to a group of boys of my own age. They would be my companions now. I found it impossible to think that they would ever be friends.

When I took my seat they looked at me curiously, but at first said nothing. I had the opportunity to look around me. As I had expected, I was unsuitably dressed. The linen tunic with the woven border, which had been fine enough for the Two Islands, was no better than a servant would wear here. All around me were silks, embroidery, and gold ornaments in bewildering profusion. *Well*, I thought, *I can't help it*, but I felt conspicuous. In any case, I looked so different from these Tar-Askans, tall and fair where I was slight and dark, that I would have given anything not to stand out among them even more. It was my appearance that finally drew the others' attention to me.

There were two of them sitting opposite me who had been giving me covert glances from the beginning of the meal. At last one of them addressed me directly.

"What are you doing here?"

"You know what he's doing here." His companion broke in, before I had a chance to reply. "He's from . . . whatever the place is called. He doesn't look like one of us, does he? He's our hostage."

"Then what is he doing here?" the first speaker persisted. He had a thin, spiteful face. "His people are slaves. He's a slave. He even looks like one. Why is he sitting here with us?"

I stopped looking for a chance to speak. I could recognize when I was being baited. I tried to ignore it, concentrating on the food. But I could not ignore the voices.

"Look, Idric," his companion began. He was heavier, slow

moving, remarkably handsome if you disregarded his sullen expression. "He's to live with us and train with us. Arax said so. He's a king's son."

"A king's son!" Idric repeated. "Then why aren't you showing him proper respect, Torac? You should be on your knees." He turned to me again. "I do beg your pardon, my lord," he said. "Some of us here are not aware of your exalted rank."

There was nothing to say to that, and my silence seemed to irritate him. His tones grew more vicious.

"A king's son? There is no king in the Two Islands—not any more. Largh rules there in the name of Askar."

"And you're no better than a slave," Torac added triumphantly.

Somehow I managed to hang on to self-control. I knew I would be doing exactly what they wanted if I broke down into anger, or worse, tears. I ate what I could from the dish in front of me, which was rich and unfamiliar. Eventually they got tired of tormenting me and went on to talk about the coming war with Kerraven. I knew I ought to listen and learn, but at first I could not concentrate. When I had myself under better control again, I realized they were discussing Arax.

"I heard he will have command over a ship," Idric was saying.

"And he'll choose his own men," Torac added.

"Well, you needn't think he'll choose you—not after that last leopard hunt."

There was laughter around the table and Torac flushed angrily. Idric had clearly touched a sore spot.

"He might not choose you, either," he rejoined. "He doesn't even like you. If you think he'll ask you to swear brotherhood with him, you can think again."

They're not even friends with each other, I thought. I felt a little better until I reflected that whatever their own quarrels might be, they were united against me. By the end of the meal I had still not spoken a word to any of them.

When I left the dining hall there was no servant to guide me, and I was nervous of asking. I thought I could find my own way back to my room, but after half an hour of wandering through seemingly identical courtyards, I had to admit that I was lost. Now that I would have asked someone, there was no one about. I was very tired. I sat on a low wall beside a bed of flowers that I was sure I had passed at least twice before and wondered what to do. I supposed I could complete a disastrous day by sleeping in the open. I had decided that after all I must go on, when a dark figure whisked noiselessly around a bend in the path and almost fell over me. I put out a hand and realized the newcomer was a girl.

She was small and brown-haired, wearing a dark dress, and was barefoot, which explained her silent approach. She had cried out sharply when she came upon me, but quickly recovered herself.

"What are you doing?" she asked irritably. "Sitting out here in the middle of nowhere, just where anybody can trip over you? Haven't you got anything better to do?"

"I'm sorry," I said.

She peered at me more closely. "Here, I don't know you, do I—oh, yes, I do!" She took a sudden step backward. "You're the lord from the Two Islands. You must be. You only came today, and I heard them talking about you. And now I suppose you'll call the steward and have me whipped."

"Why should I do that?"

"Well, I haven't exactly spoken respectfully to you, have I? Though if you want to be treated like a lord, you should try to look like one."

"It doesn't matter," I said awkwardly. "I won't have you whipped. Don't be afraid."

"Oh, I'm not afraid. I would rather not be whipped, obviously." She looked down at me where I was still sitting on the wall. "Then excuse me, my lord, but what are you doing here?"

"I couldn't find my room," I confessed, feeling stupid.

"Oh, is that all! Come on, I'll show you. They said they were putting you in the Fountain Court."

Before I could rise, she stooped suddenly and lifted the cross I wore around my neck.

"That's Kerravene work."

"Yes."

She let the cross fall, and I thought her hand was shaking slightly.

"I come from there," she said abruptly. "Come on."

I followed her down the path. It occurred to me that she was the first woman I had seen in Tar-Askar. Even in the great hall and the dining room, all those present had been men—even the servants. For the sake of something to say, I asked her why.

"Women live apart in Tar-Askar," she explained, "in the court, that is. The women's quarters are over there." She gestured vaguely. "The women hardly ever come here, except for the slaves."

"Are you a slave?" I asked, shocked.

She stopped dead and turned on me, her eyes blazing.

"Well, what did you think I was?"

"I—I'm sorry. I didn't know."

She seemed to relax a little and went on through the passage into the next courtyard.

"No, I don't suppose you did," she went on at last. "I was a fisherman's daughter in Kerraven. We were raided. I was brought here. That's all."

"Almost like me," I said quietly.

"But you're not a slave, are you?"

"No."

I wanted to say, "But I'm a prisoner. I can't go home." But it sounded self-pitying, and I knew she would despise that. I could feel there was anger in her, but no self-pity. I found myself admiring her, and I wanted her to like me. She was the first person who had spoken to me as if I were a human being.

"What's your name?" I asked.

"Meriu. And you're Aurion. They told me that. I suppose I should say 'my lord.' "

"I wish you wouldn't."

She gave me a look, but said nothing. A moment later we passed through into another courtyard and she stopped.

"Here you are."

I recognized the door of my room.

"Thank you."

I hesitated. I did not know what to say to her, but I did not want her to go without some idea that I might see her again. We stood looking at each other for a moment and it was Meriu who broke the silence.

"Then you worship the true God in the Two Islands?"

"Yes."

"In Kerraven, too. But here—there's no one else, Aurion, no one at all. . . ."

Her voice quivered a little. It sounded so different from her previous sharpness, that I reached out and took her hand.

"There are two of us now," I said.

She snatched her hand away almost as soon as I had touched it.

"We'll talk again," she said, and vanished into the darkness.

5

On the following morning, another servant woke me and told me he was to be my regular attendant. He was no older than I. He was small for a Tar-Askan, with a tendency to chatter, dutifully repressed, but never far from the surface. His name was Hithiel. He had brought my breakfast—bread and fruit and a hot, spiced drink. Hithiel told me that the evening meal was the only one taken by all the court together. Feeling relieved by that, and refreshed by a night's sleep, I was able to enjoy breakfast. With the sun slanting in through my window, I looked forward to the day ahead without too much apprehension.

When I had finished eating, Hithiel told me that I should report to the practice ground for a training session. As soon as I was ready, he showed me where to go. The ground was still within the outer wall of the palace, but on a much lower level, down many flights of steps from the living quarters. On the way I recognized the dining hall and the main entrance to the great hall. I began to hope that I would not get lost again.

One place I did not recognize was a large, domed building within its own retaining wall. We passed an archway through which I could see a courtyard and guards in scarlet tunics flanking a pair of ornamented bronze doors.

"What is that?" I asked Hithiel.

"That is the temple of Askar, my lord," he replied. He touched a hand to his forehead as the god's name passed his lips.

I did not ask any more.

The practice ground was also walled off, entered by an arched passageway. Within the thickness of the wall were tiny rooms used as weapon stores. Hithiel took his leave outside, and

I walked through the arch. I was standing at the top of a shallow flight of steps leading down to a sand-covered arena. Several people were already there. I recognized some of my supper companions of the night before. They were in pairs, practicing with swords. An older man, thickset and gray-haired, was shouting instructions. At first no one noticed me.

I was still hesitating when a voice spoke at my shoulder.

"Well, well! The Lord of the Two Islands!"

I turned. It was Idric, the thin-faced boy who had spoken to me at supper. He made an elaborate, mocking bow.

"Good morning, my lord."

"Good morning."

"And you're to join us for practice! We're honored. Aren't we honored, Torac?" he added as his friend and some of the others came up.

"We'd better see what he can do," Torac said.

"Come on," Idric invited.

I turned to go down the steps, but as I did so I felt his foot hook around my ankle. A second later I found myself sprawling at the bottom. I sat up in the midst of humiliating laughter.

"You'll never make a warrior if you can't stay on your feet," Torac said.

I tried to stand, but a blow on my back sent me flying again. The next time I was more watchful. It was Torac who approached me. As he reached out, I grabbed his arm and pulled him down with me. For a few moments we wrestled in the sand, but he was stronger and more skillful. Soon I was helpless under his weight, his hands at my throat. My senses were spiraling away.

Suddenly I was released. My vision cleared and the pounding in my ears gradually died away. I was able to sit up. As I did so, I was aware of a voice, and of someone standing at the top of the steps. With a shock I realized it was Arax.

". . . brawling like a crowd of drunken goat-keepers," he was saying when I had recovered enough to listen. His voice was blisteringly angry. "If this is Tar-Askan nobility, may the great Askar help us all! And as for showing courtesy to a guest within our walls—"

CHAPTER 5

He sprang down and offered a hand to help me up without interrupting the flow of his speech. It occurred to me, in the midst of being grateful to him, that he had not shown much courtesy himself on the day before.

"I should expect to find more courtesy in a fisherman's hut." His glance raked across them, the sea-green eyes snapping. Torac, brushing sand from his tunic close by, muttered something inaudible.

"And as for you, Torac," Arax went on scathingly, "his ancestors were kings when yours were trapping frogs in the marshes."

Someone snickered and Torac looked sullenly furious.

"So why are you standing here gaping? Do you want the Kerravene warriors to cut you into ribbons?"

They dispersed hurriedly and returned to the exercise with the swords. Arax stayed beside me. Looking down at me, he was laughing.

"Well, little cousin?"

"Thank you, my lord."

"Don't thank me. I enjoyed it. They bore me, Aurion, they bore me to screaming. Wait."

He darted back toward the weapon stores, and returned a moment later with a sword in each hand. The blade flashed as he tossed one to me; startled, I managed to catch it.

"Now!"

He cried out the word as he leaped down the steps again to face me, and I automatically raised the sword to parry his stroke.

"Too slow—no, keep going . . . like that!"

He was attacking, testing, and teaching me all at once. And as I tried to defend myself against his onslaught, I had no time to think about anything else. As he fought, he issued a stream of instructions. Though where he found breath for it I could not tell.

"Keep the sword up. Watch your feet—no, don't *watch* your feet, idiot—that's better."

Somehow I managed to keep up with him. It was almost exhilarating. I felt I was doing quite well. I did not realize he was holding back for me until at last he threw aside restraint; suddenly, without knowing how, I was disarmed and flat on my back on the sand. Arax was pinning me down, laughing once again.

"If I were your enemy, you would be dead." He hauled me to my feet. "But it wasn't bad for a first try. We'll make a warrior of you yet, little cousin."

Then he seemed to lose interest in me. He turned me over to the instructor before strolling over to challenge Idric. While I attended to the instructor's more conventional lesson, I thought over his last words. It had not occurred to me that if the war with Kerraven took place, I would be ordered to fight—and on what was for me, the wrong side. But Arax's words clearly implied it. I did not want to take sword against Kerraven, where they worshiped the true God and were friendly to my father and the Two Islands, but if I stayed in Tar-Askar, I would have no choice. And it was not much consolation that I would certainly be killed before I had the chance to do much harm. It was one more reason telling me that I had to stop the war.

When the training was over we washed in another bathhouse beside the practice ground. I realized I should have brought a clean tunic. The one I had been wearing was filthy. Before I left, hoping to change as quickly as possible, Arax came over to me again.

"We're going swimming tonight," he announced. "Do you want to come?"

I had not expected that. My first reaction was to make an excuse, but Arax interrupted me.

"We're going to swim across the bay, have supper there, and camp for the night. Then in the morning we swim back. Come with us." His eyes glinted at me. "You can swim, can't you?"

"Yes, I can," I said, stung. "I'll come."

And then I began to wonder what I had gotten myself into.

6

Long before the evening, I was wishing I had never agreed to accompany Arax and the others on their night excursion. I should have been encouraged, for at least Arax had thought to invite me. But I could not be sure about his motives. On our first meeting he had tried to frighten and humiliate me. On our second he had helped me. I could not know what he would take into his head to do next. He was too unaccountable. I could not trust him.

I spent the afternoon alone, exploring the court, and half hoping to see Meriu. She was nowhere to be found. I did not know what her duties were, and I certainly could not take the step of sending for her. So I had nothing to occupy my mind except the approaching evening. By the time I went down to the beach I was feeling very apprehensive.

Before we parted that morning Arax had shown me where to go—through one of the gates in the outer wall of the palace that led out on to a strip of beach. I was half hoping that they might have gone without me. But when I arrived they were all there. Arax acknowledged my presence with a lifted hand, but did not come to speak to me. Feeling awkward, I waited.

I had seen the bay when I arrived by ship, but never before from this angle. The king's palace was built on the hillside along the eastern arm, and beyond it was the little town of fishermen and craftsmen that supplied the palace. Farther along to my left, I could just see the boats of the fishing fleet. Several figures moved amongst them as their owners made ready for the night's fishing. Across the bay the sun was going down behind wooded hills. The sea blazed scarlet, broken at one point by a black pinnacle of rock. Everything was very quiet; even the talk of my companions seemed hushed.

I tensed as I realized Idric was beside me. I expected further taunting, but when he spoke his voice was quite amiable.

"We're headed for the point over there," he told me. "The shortest way is to keep the rock on your right."

"I see."

He rejoined the others, and I wondered what had made him tell me that. He had never shown friendliness before, and his remark about the rock was so obvious that it scarcely needed saying. As the first of the swimmers began to leave, Arax came across the beach toward me.

"What did Idric say to you?" he asked.

I told him and watched as his face darkened. At first I thought it was me he was angry with.

"Keep the rock on your left. It's further," he explained, "but go the other way and you'll be caught in a current. It sets out to sea, and that's the last anyone would see of you—unless the fishing fleet picked you up."

He turned and glanced at Idric, who by now was wading out into the sea. I was glad he was not looking like that at me, but he said nothing, and I could not think of anything to say. Then he faced me again.

"Look, Aurion," he began, without the playful, rather patronizing air that I was having to get used to, "are you sure about this? I'll stay with you, but you'll only feel ashamed if I have to fish you out."

"You won't have to. And you don't need to stay with me."

Illogically, I was beginning to be angry myself. I would rather have him hostile than starting to feel sorry for me. He grinned.

"Have it your own way."

He turned his back on me, slid out of his tunic and left it lying. Then he ran down into the water. Feeling that somehow I had said or done the wrong thing, I followed him, last of all.

Once I had begun to swim, most of my problems left me. Children in the Two Islands swim before they walk, and I loved it. I had not swum since before the Tar-Askan ship came, so I could not help but enjoy it—the cool, silken water, the dying light around me, and my own skill, which no one—even here—could find fault with. I remembered to keep the rock on my left, but the ugly little incident with Idric refused to stay in my mind. I was as near to being happy as I had been since I left my home.

Eventually I could hear waves on the further beach. I began to wonder exactly where I should come ashore, for the sun had gone by now. Treading water, I looked ahead and could see red sparks in the darkness—fires on the beach, I realized. Then there was splashing and a head in the water beside me: Arax.

"I apologize, little cousin," he said, playful as ever. "Race to the beach?"

He won, but not by much. I could not help feeling satisfaction, and more so when Idric arrived. He was obviously much more tired than I was. I know it was childish, but it was a comfort to prove there was at least one thing I could do well.

Arax led me to one of the fires where there were towels and dry clothes.

"We sent servants around the bay with carts this afternoon," he explained. "Supper should be ready soon."

I surprised myself by feeling hungry, and the bowl of hot soup that was served to me soon after was very welcome. Somehow I found myself sitting around a fire with Arax and two or three of the others, not saying much, but listening to their talk. I felt part of the circle, accepted. The food, cooked over the fires, was much more to my taste than the elaborate meal of the night before. I found myself hoping that I had crossed some sort of line, and would find things easier from now on.

At last the talk began to die down, and we prepared for sleep. The night was so warm and clear that we could lie on the ground in the open with no more than a blanket, and that not really necessary. Arax dropped his blanket beside mine and spread it out.

"Glad you came?" he asked, smiling.

I nodded.

"We often do this," he told me, as he sat down. "It's not often such a beautiful night, though. You might almost expect Askar himself to come out of the sea."

He touched his forehead as Hithiel had done when he named the god. Something must have shown in my face, for his own grew colder and he said, "But you don't believe that."

"No."

"My father told me. You believe in a god who died. How can a god die?"

This was my opportunity, and I prayed for the right words.

"The God I believe in lived as a man—not here, but on the other world we all came from once."

"So they say."

"It's what my father taught me. Men from our home world came and settled on all the Six Worlds. But later on, somehow, we lost touch, and now no one knows how to find our home world again."

Arax shrugged.

"Then if that's so, your god belongs there, not here."

"No. Don't you see, Arax? He's God of everywhere—our home world, and here on Ocean, and all the Six Worlds."

"But he died. He let his enemies kill him."

"Yes," I tried to explain. "He died and came to life again because He had to save us from all the wrong we do, and so—"

He interrupted me.

"Askar would not let his enemies kill him." He was angry now, with me or with what I had said. "Askar defeats his enemies. He will help us defeat Kerraven, and then you'll see how much power that crazy god of yours has to stop him."

He rolled himself in his blanket and refused to say any more. The harmony of the evening was broken, and I knew I was no closer to carrying out my task. After a while I lay down too, but it was a long time before I could sleep.

7

The next day, after the swim back across the bay in the early morning, I met Meriu again. When I returned to the Fountain Court on the way to my room, she was in the garden, picking flowers and placing them in a reed basket. She looked different, more self-controlled, the flyaway brown hair braided neatly around her head, and as I came toward her she smiled at me.

"Enjoy your swim?" she asked.

"How do you know I've been swimming?"

"Your hair's wet. In any case, I heard you went with Arax and the others. How did you get on?"

I shrugged. "They don't like me."

"Did you expect them to?"

"No. But it would be easier. . . . You know, Meriu, I really thought Arax was starting to be more friendly, last night. Then I tried to talk to him about God, but he didn't want to listen. He's hardly spoken to me since."

Meriu looked at me. There was a sudden bitterness in her face that faded slowly.

"No, they won't listen," she said with a sigh. "I've tried, but of course, no one listens to a slave, and a woman at that. You might do better, but I wouldn't start with Arax if I were you."

"Why not?"

"He's a Tar-Askan warrior, or he likes to think he is. What does he want with a God of peace?"

"But, Meriu, I must try. Listen and I'll tell you what my father said before I left the Two Islands." We sat on the edge of the fountain and I told her about the coming war with Kerraven, and how my father thought it might be stopped. Meriu shook her head.

"You would need the support of someone really important," she said. "The king himself—or yes, Arax. But they'll never change."

"I've prayed about it. If there is a way, God will show me."

Meriu reached out her hand toward the fountain. It was a stone dolphin spouting a thin stream of water that fell into the basin with a cool, pleasant sound. Water splashed over her fingers.

"It's so beautiful here," she said. "And cruel. But it's easy to forget the cruelty. Aurion, don't be . . . don't be led away by it. Don't start to live their way."

I did not really understand her.

"I won't." I replied. "But why—"

"You have to be with them," she said. "You have to do what they do. And he fascinates you—Arax. I can tell by the way you talk about him. He's stronger than you, Aurion. He could bend you to his way."

"But Meriu—" I protested.

She interrupted me by springing to her feet and taking up her basket again.

"I can't waste time chattering to you," she said. "I've work to do."

She set off down a path. I followed and caught up to her as she stopped to choose more flowers.

"I'll help you."

She gave me a crooked smile. "No Tar-Askan lord would be seen dead picking flowers."

"I'm not a Tar-Askan lord." To prove it I broke off a spray of the white bells she was picking and laid it in her basket.

"Not yet," was her only response.

I saw nothing more of Arax until that evening. Toward the end of the meal, he came over to the table where I was sitting with the others.

"Leopard hunt tomorrow," he announced. "It's about time you had some real exercise."

Chapter 7

His glance went around and fell on me, and he came to stand beside me.

"Aurion, little cousin." He was smiling, delighted by something, but not friendly. "Have you ever hunted leopard?"

"No, my lord. We have none in the Two Islands."

"Then you have a treat in store. Can you ride?"

"Yes, my lord. At least, I—"

He broke in. "Then sunrise, in the main courtyard. I'll find you a horse and a spear. Don't be late. I might be very angry if you were late."

He turned away and left after a word or two with some of the others. I went back to my room. It occurred to me not to join the hunt at all, for I was apprehensive and Arax's last words had irritated me. I wondered what he or anyone else could do if I did not appear at the meeting place. I did not really want to find out. And Meriu's words returned to me, rather uncomfortably. Was I really fascinated by Arax? In that case, it might be better to do as he said, rather than draw his attention to me by disobeying. I sighed. Of course I had never seriously contemplated doing anything else.

When I arrived early the next morning, the main courtyard seemed full of men and horses. I could see Arax already mounted on a fiery black. He must have been looking out for me, because he wheeled toward me at once. He sat looking down at me, controlling the restless horse with perfect ease.

"Good morning, little cousin. Looking forward to the hunt?"

"No, my lord."

He grinned at that, as if he were genuinely amused.

"Oh, you'll enjoy yourself. We all enjoy ourselves."

I doubted that, and let my doubt show, but Arax took no notice. He snapped his fingers at a groom who led up another horse, a chestnut, that looked as spirited as Arax's own. My heart sank. In the Two Islands, as I had tried to explain to Arax the night before, I had ridden hill ponies—stocky little beasts that would carry you for hours, or days if need be, uncomplainingly, but were not built for speed. We had no horses such as these. Of course, Arax knew. This was another test, another opportunity for my humiliation. Still, I had rejected his help, honestly offered, over the swimming. I could hardly expect him to be helpful now.

I took a breath and mounted. For the first minutes I felt unsteady and a long way from the ground. Someone thrust a spear into my hand, which made it even more difficult to manage the horse. Somehow I stayed in control. By the time the gates were opened and the hunting party began to move off, I began to hope that I would not disgrace myself. I brought my horse into line somewhere near the rear, while at the head of the column, Arax led the way into the hills.

8

The road we took at first followed the curve of the bay, but soon it divided and we took the right fork into the hills. We began to climb. The road moved back and forth across the hillside, always with a steep slope falling away below us. The sun rose higher and the day grew hot. Although we were shielded from direct sunlight by trees and riotous undergrowth, a steamy, uncomfortable heat built up around us. My tunic was clinging to me. I thought longingly of the cool shock of a plunge into the waters of the bay.

About midmorning we passed a small village of wooden huts clinging to the side of the hill. After that the path led into a narrow, upland valley, sparsely wooded with steep hills on either side. The air was clearer here. I could feel the movement of a faint breeze. Once we were well into the valley we stopped and dismounted; grooms took charge of the horses. We rested briefly and passed around food and drink.

No one took much notice of me. Idric and Torac, who had been my chief tormentors, now ignored me completely. I wondered if perhaps Arax had spoken to them, but I decided that I was making my own affairs too important. Arax probably never thought about me when I was out of his sight.

He had not forgotten me now, however. He came over to me as the rest of the party were getting ready to move off.

"Leopard country," he said, gesturing up the valley. "We'll have good sport today. I can feel it."

He stood silent for a moment, peering ahead into the light woodland.

"He's there," he said softly. "I know he's there. Watching us, maybe. Still in hiding, but not for long."

Then he turned back to me, smiling faintly, and tested my spear point with his thumb.

"Don't try throwing that, little cousin," he advised. "Keep it to defend yourself if you need to. Better still, keep out of the way."

Before I could reply, he moved off to take his place at the head of the group.

We all walked slowly, watchfully, in a line that straggled roughly across the width of the valley. We kept pace with each other except for Arax and one or two others trying to emulate him—Idric among them—who moved ahead. Sometimes we lost sight of each other among the trees. The wood was quiet, but not silent. I could hear the alarm calls of birds as we approached. There were unexplained rustlings in the undergrowth and the sound of my own footsteps on last year's dry leaves. Now and again a low-voiced cry was heard from one hunter to another.

The sun shone strongly now as it was approaching noon. Sunlight poured through the trees to make a shifting, dappled pattern on the woodland floor. We walked in a world of green and gold and brown. It was very peaceful. Then through the trees I heard a rustling crash, a sharp cry of exultation—Arax, I was sure—and through it all a low, continuous snarling.

I broke into a run, through the trees and toward the sound. Others converged on the place. We came out into a clearing. Arax was there, his back to me, poised with the spear in his hand. Facing him was a creature that looked as if the gold-brown of the forest had taken on a body that was lithe, beautiful, and deadly.

I stopped. I had no breath to cry out. I was part of a wide circle with Arax and the leopard at its center.

"Keep back," he said quietly, never taking his eyes from his adversary. "This is mine."

Briefly they circled, as if they were locked together in some kind of dance. I remembered how I had seen Arax at our first meeting, with the threatening grace of the fighting cat. And now, watching them together, I realized the kinship again. But all that went through my mind in seconds. The next instant, the leopard sprang.

Arax took it full on his spear and held it writhing, the great paws slashing at air. I could see his face now. It was exalted—in another world. Then he was on the ground, struggling to reach his hunting knife in the midst of a storm of claws. I did not realize what had happened until I saw the broken spear shaft trailing from the leopard's shoulder.

For the space of a breath I looked around. None of the others moved. Then I flung myself forward, drove my spear into the leopard's flank, and unprepared for the power in its body, lost my footing as it twisted and bore down on me. Desperately I clung to the spear, knowing it would be death to lose my grip on it. I could feel the creature's breath against my face. Then the powerful body went limp, falling half across me. I pushed it off and sat up to see Arax drawing his hunting knife out of the neck.

He turned away to clean the blade of his knife in the grass. I got to my feet, tugged out the spear, and did the same. I did not know what to say to him or what he would say to me. But when I turned back and found him facing me across the body, it was to meet the one reaction I had not expected—cold, furious anger.

"I told you to keep back."

His voice was quiet, venomous.

"But, Arax—"

"The leopard was mine. How dare you come between me and my leopard?"

"It would have killed you."

He moved around the dead animal and put his hands on my shoulders. The touch was light. I should have been less terrified if he had hurt me.

"You have disgraced me. No one does that to me twice, Aurion."

"Arax, I'm sorry . . . but the spear . . ."

My voice stumbled into silence at the look in his eyes. He took a step backward and jerked the spear out of my hand.

"Get out of here," he said. "Get out of my sight. Go home."

He turned away from me. Without another word to him,

without looking at the others, I went. As I retreated, I heard someone behind me give way to unsteady laughter.

I returned to the end of the valley where the horses were waiting. Fortunately a Tar-Askan groom would never dream of asking a Tar-Askan lord to explain his actions. I collected my horse with no more than a word or two between us. I was on the hill path when reaction set in, and I found myself shaking. I did not know whether I wanted to shout in anger, or weep, or turn my horse onto some other road so I should never have to return to the court and face Arax again. Bitter homesickness swept over me. I thought it would have been easier if the leopard had killed me.

Perhaps because I was so shaken, I let the horse take the downhill path too quickly, only realizing when it stumbled. I kept my seat and dragged sharply on the reins. The horse tossed its head up, half rearing, and missed its footing on the edge of the path. I was thrown outward. As the horse scrambled to safety, the bridle gave way under my weight and I fell. I cried out. I crashed through thin vegetation that scarcely helped to break my fall. Then something struck the back of my head. I knew nothing more.

9

I opened my eyes, saw nothing but blurred green and specks of sunlight and tried to sit up. Pain seared through my head. I fell back again, closing my eyes. As I lay still, I began to remember where I was and how I had come there. After a while, more cautiously, I tried to sit up again. By the time I had managed it, with my back against a tree, I was sick and near to fainting again. But I hung on to consciousness and looked around me.

I was at the bottom of a slope, close to a trickle of water that snaked its way in and out of tree roots until it was lost to sight. Above my head must be the road I had been traveling, but I could not see it. The light that penetrated the trees was golden, slanting, as if the sun were close to setting. I must have been lying there several hours.

I began to realize that night could not be far off and that I must be out of the forest before then. Judging that I dared not wait any longer, I started to get to my feet. A moment later I had sunk back against the tree again, fighting off the waves of nausea that followed the pain when I tried to put weight on my right foot. I had sprained it, perhaps worse, in the fall. I was helpless, and night would come soon.

For a few minutes I admit I gave way to fear. It was all I could do not to break down into tears. I knew I should pray, but terror stifled it. Every rustle in the undergrowth was a snake or another leopard. Every shrub might be hiding the flicker of hostile eyes. I tried calling for help, but only silence answered.

After a while I managed to pull myself out of my panic. I was armed against attack; I wore my hunting knife. And I remembered the village. It was not far away—at the head of the valley. If I could reach it, they would give me shelter for the night and send a message in the morning.

All that was sensible, but it was still beyond my powers. Pain stabbed through my head when I tried to move, and my right foot was useless. My right arm was marked with deep scratches from shoulder to wrist and had bled, though the bleeding had stopped. That must have been the leopard. I hadn't noticed it until now. With all the determination I could gather, I set myself to crawl, slowly and painfully, up the slope. Before long I had to give in and collapse, shaking and once again clinging to consciousness. It would have been easier just to let myself slip back into darkness, but I knew that if I did that, my last chance would have gone.

Then as I lay there, I could not help noticing a clump of flowers that grew inches from my face. They were blue, star-shaped, with broad, dark leaves. I half sat up, picked one, and sniffed its pungent, not unpleasant scent. It was starweed. It grew in the Two Islands, and an infusion of the leaves was an excellent cure for headaches. Even in my present situation, I could not avoid seeing the funny side of that. But my half smile was followed by a renewal of homesickness when I remembered how my father had taught me his craft of healing, how to recognize and prepare the herbs he used and what sicknesses each one would cure.

Since I had traveled to Tar-Askar, I had put the healer's craft right out of my mind. Now I wondered how I could have been so stupid. That was a skill I had no reason to be ashamed of. It was a way of being useful. There must be healers in Tar-Askar whom I could help. Perhaps I would have knowledge from the Two Islands that I could share with them.

By now I was sitting up again, looking around to see what other plants grew there. Almost at once I noticed another—gray-leaved, yellow-flowered, creeping over a nearby stone. That was used to prevent infection in wounds. And too far away for me to be sure was a shrub with fine pointed leaves that was good for all kinds of fevers. The hills of Tar-Askar were a storehouse of healing herbs! As I began to plan what I would do, I failed to notice the dying of the sunlight. It came as a shock to hear my name being called from the path above my head.

It was, of course, Arax. When I replied, he came sliding down through the undergrowth, using his spear for balance, apparently indifferent to the steep slope and the possibility of falling.

"What have you been up to?" he asked.

He seemed perfectly restored to good humor. My fears of facing him again receded.

"I fell," I explained. "I'm sorry, Arax. How did you find me?"

"We overtook your horse, grazing along by the bay. There was no sign of you, so I came back."

"Thank you."

He shrugged, smiling.

"Think nothing of it. You know, you won a bet for me with Idric. He thought you would be panicking when I found you. 'Sobbing like a little girl' was what he said, I think. And instead here you are, quite cool and composed, picking flowers."

I realized I was still holding the blue flower. I tossed it away, feeling rather embarrassed.

"No Tar-Askan lord would be seen dead picking flowers," I murmured, quoting Meriu.

Arax burst out laughing.

"Idric certainly wouldn't," he said. He held out a hand to me. "But if you've quite finished, we should be on our way."

Even with his help, it was all I could do to stand. I did not see how I was going to climb the slope. Rather incoherently, I tried to explain to him and apologize, but he interrupted me.

"Don't fuss, little cousin. There's nothing to worry about."

And somehow it was possible. Slowly we struggled back toward the path. In the midst of all the pain and effort, I was determined that I was not going to disgrace myself in front of him, and when we finally stood on level ground again, I felt a sudden glow of satisfaction at the thought that he was pleased with me.

The horses were there, Arax's and my own, tethered to a low branch. Arax helped me mount.

"Are you sure you can ride?" he asked. "I can take you up with me if you would rather."

"No—no, I'll be all right."

We set off through gathering darkness. My horse followed Arax's. The horse was quite docile now, perhaps because it was tired. All I had to do was concentrate on staying on his back. By the time we reached the palace, even that was quite enough. And when a groom had taken the horses back to the stables, I realized there were still several flights of steps between me and my room. I was almost too exhausted to face them.

"What about the steps?" Arax asked, as if reading my thoughts. "I don't really think I could carry you. Not after a day like this. Shall I call someone?"

I shook my head.

"I can manage it if you help me."

So we toiled together up flights of steps that seemed endless, glimmering white in the light of the rising moon, until at last we came to the Fountain Court. My room was empty, and in darkness. Arax helped me to a seat, and went to light the lamp.

"Shall I put you to bed, little cousin?" he asked teasingly.

I protested something, suddenly embarrassed again. He remained bending over the lamp, coaxing the flame. I saw for the first time that his shoulders and his chest were covered with scratches—the claw marks of the leopard, at least one of which was deep enough to be still oozing blood.

"Arax," I said, "I'm sorry—about the leopard."

He did not look at me. After a moment he said abruptly, "I'm sorry, too."

"I didn't understand."

By now the flame was burning steadily. He straightened up and faced me.

"It's a custom," he explained, "a fight to the death, man against beast. Of course, you didn't know." He smiled, with an odd touch of bitterness. "The others all did as they were told. They would have watched and carried my body home with honor, telling everyone how I died nobly, taking my leopard." He shrugged. "Well, it's a point of view."

CHAPTER 9

"And now you're dishonored."

His smile lost the bitter touch.

"No, not really. Just unfortunate to have my glorious death prevented by some idiot from the Two Islands. And to tell you the truth, Aurion, quite glad not to be a dead hero."

He stood looking down at me for a moment, and then turned and went swiftly to the door.

"I'll call your servant," he said and vanished into the darkness.

I remained where I was, waiting. Although I did not understand his abrupt departure, I felt an unfamiliar warmth at the words that had led up to it. He was not angry any longer. He understood what I had done. I hardly dared believe it, but I thought that perhaps he was becoming my friend.

10

The next morning I had a visit from Meriu. She set down a full water jar by my bed, and herself, just as composedly, at its foot.

"What have you been up to?" she asked.

"How did you know I was hurt?"

"I heard." She waved her hand impatiently and then added, even more irritably, "In the slaves' courtyard—nothing but gossip, gossip, gossip! As if we hadn't anything better to do."

I smiled. Somehow her downright manner always made me feel better.

"Then you must have heard what happened."

She leaned over and peered at the claw marks on my arm. "You obviously got into an argument with something."

"It was a leopard. But that isn't all that happened."

I told her about the leopard hunt and the accident with the horse on my way home. I did leave out what Arax had said to me before he left, for I had the idea that Meriu did not like the thought of friendship between myself and Arax. She was, of course, unimpressed by the story.

"I always said Tar-Askan men were fools." Then, more briskly, she went on, "Is there anything I can do for you?"

There was something that had been on my mind ever since I had spoken to Hithiel the night before. I was glad to have the chance to ask Meriu.

"Yes. Tell me—is there a healer in the court? I tried to ask my servant last night, but he didn't seem to understand what I was talking about. And it didn't seem as if he wanted to discuss it."

"I'm not surprised. Here the healers are the priests of Askar."

"Oh."

I was beginning to understand.

"Then it's just as well that I can do without them, I suppose. Well . . . I couldn't ask, could I?"

"No."

That was without question. If I were to bring anyone in Tar-Askar to the knowledge of the true God, the last thing I could do was ask for help from the priests of Askar.

"Not that they do much healing," Meriu went on. "Perhaps an incantation to the god. . . . But you're not badly hurt, are you, Aurion? Bad enough to need a healer?"

"No. No, I'm not. But my foot needs bandaging properly, and I have a splitting headache. . . ."

I leaned forward and winced. The sudden movement had been inadvisable.

"Listen, Meriu, I'm a healer myself, or I was, in the Two Islands. If you could get a bandage, I could show you what to do with it. And yesterday I saw a plant growing—but no. I was forgetting. You have your duties. They might not let you go and look for it."

Meriu sniffed. "Aurion, I'm a slave and you're a king's son. If you tell me to go, I go. And I'd be glad to get out of here for an hour or two. What does this plant look like?"

Later that day Meriu brought the bandage and put it on as skillfully as she did everything. And she found starweed, the blue-flowered plant, growing on the edge of the forest not far from the palace. I showed her how to make the infusion, and my headache subsided.

As the days passed I grew more disturbed that Arax did not come to visit me. I began to think that I had mistaken his friendliness on the night of the leopard hunt. He had his own friends; he led a busy life and had no reason to think about me when I was not there.

I tried to put him out of my mind and concentrated instead on my plans to use my healing skills in Tar-Askar. It was something I could do that would be useful. And if the king gave me permission, I meant to ask for Meriu as my assistant and pupil. She would be quick to learn, and I thought she would be happier than as a palace drudge.

When I finally left my room, my foot was still not strong enough to return to training. Instead, I explored further in the court, walked in the gardens, and sat in the sun on a terrace where I could look out over the sea. Meriu came with me as often as she could get away. I saw Arax occasionally, at a distance, or on the high table at the evening meal, but he never spoke to me.

I was on the terrace one morning, watching a ship working its way into the bay. It was a merchant ship with patched white sails. It reminded me that except for the warship that had brought me to Tar-Askar, I had seen no other ships. It puzzled me, and I asked Meriu, who was sitting beside me, for an explanation.

"This is the king's palace," she pointed out, with a pitying look for my ignorance. "He doesn't want to live in the middle of a shipyard. A few miles up the coast—" she gestured—"there's a whole town, mostly of shipwrights. They're preparing for war, Aurion. They launched a new warship the other day. The king rode up there and sailed back in it. It's gone now, though, training a new crew."

"Did Arax go?" I asked.

"No. Why?"

I felt ashamed. I had seized on that as a possible reason why he had not come to see me.

"Nothing. Only I heard someone say he was to have command of a ship."

I made myself come to terms with what Meriu's news really meant. One more warship was one more reason for Tar-Askar to declare war on Kerraven and to win. I did not know how much time I had left to turn some of the Tar-Askans away from war, and so far I had done nothing. I felt a sudden sense of urgency. I prayed quickly now, informally, for God to show me what I should do. But there seemed to be no answer, no way out of my inactivity except for my plan to practice my skills as a healer. I wondered if that might possibly be the answer. Unlikely as it seemed, God might have chosen that route for me to carry out my task. Later that day I requested an audience with the king.

He received me the following morning. Hithiel brought the message, rather awestruck by it, and conducted me not to the great hall, but to the king's private apartments. It was in a sparsely furnished reception room, plain by Tar-Askan standards, where Largh, the king, was already waiting for me.

I knelt before him. As he had done on the first day, he left me there while he looked me over. Once again I was aware of the formidable power that was in him. Then he motioned for me to rise, and went to sit in a raised chair at the other end of the room.

"You are recovered from you injuries?" he asked.

"Yes, my lord. Thank you."

"My son told me what happened. You both behaved foolishly."

The words were not spoken in the tone of a rebuke. I was a little encouraged.

"You have something to ask of me?" the king went on.

I explained to him how I had worked as a healer in the Two Islands and how it had occurred to me that I might do the same work here.

Largh listened without interrupting, but when I had finished, he said, "Here all such healing is done by the priests of Askar."

There was something odd about the way he spoke, and I had begun to reply before I realized he had not raised his hand to his forehead in the formal gesture of respect when he named the god.

"But my lord, I—"

He interrupted. "You are not suggesting, I suppose, that you wish to become a priest?"

"No, my lord."

"No. The training is long. And besides, you worship this . . . dead god. . . . Strange. No, Aurion, I cannot permit healing through the power of another god in Tar-Askar."

"But my lord, it's not—" I began, and paused, aware of difficulties. It was going to be hard for me to explain to him. I tried again. "My lord, I should pray to my God for His blessing on my work and thank Him for my skill. But the skill is my own. I could teach it to a Tar-Askan and he could use it, even if—"

"You are coming perilously close to blasphemy," the king said, interrupting me again. "Your request is denied. You may go."

There was something in his eyes that told me it would be useless and perhaps even dangerous to protest. I took my leave. On my way back to my room I prayed again that I might understand the king's refusal. I had been so sure that God had meant me to work through my healing skills. Now the way was blocked. I prayed for understanding, but if God meant to answer the prayer, He did not do so then.

11

It was evening. I had just left the dining hall at the end of supper. Arax and most of the others had not been there. I had heard that Arax was giving a party in his own rooms. A musician had arrived in the court and there was some other reason for celebration that was not very clear to me. I could not repress a small pang of envy. Of course I should have been too nervous to go to one of Arax's parties, even if he had invited me. But he had not invited me. I would like to have heard the music.

I returned slowly, discouraged in spite of myself, to the Fountain Court. On the way I paused, for I could hear very faint, but clear, the brilliant notes of a harp. Almost without deciding, I turned toward it—through another courtyard and up some steps, as if the music drew me by an invisible cord. I found myself on a terrace. I had never been here before, but I realized I was outside Arax's rooms.

I drew back into the shadows. To my right was a low wall overlooking the sea. Opposite me were open windows that blazed with light. I could hear the subdued sound of voices, and over all, the music of the harp. I was terrified of being found there.

"But I'm doing no harm," I argued with myself. "If all I do is listen—" After all, no one was likely to come and find me. The light from the windows did not reach me, and I slid down to sit on the top step in the shelter of the wall. And for a little while I was able to relax and enjoy the music.

Then it stopped. The murmur of voices rose and was mingled with laughter and the sounds of movement. I prepared to go. But before I could move, the yellow oblong of a door opened in the opposite wall and was blotted out as a tall figure stepped out on to the terrace. Arax. Now I did not dare to move, and I could only hope that he would go back inside quickly.

Instead he moved to the terrace wall and leaned against it, looking out into the night. His step was unsteady. I felt disturbed at the thought that he had been drinking too much. My eyes were used to the darkness by now, and I could see that he looked flushed. He was breathing deeply, holding his face to the cool breeze that fanned through his mane of golden hair.

I do not think I moved. But perhaps he could feel my gaze on him, for suddenly he turned.

"Who's there?"

I shrank away from the sharp question.

"Who is it? Come here!"

He took a pace toward me. In another moment I would be discovered. Better to show myself and preserve a little dignity. I stood, and faced him.

"Aurion." His voice now was quiet, puzzled. "What's the matter? Did you want me?"

I felt helplessly embarrassed, and more than that—if he had laughed at me, I might have defended myself, but there was something in this curious gentleness that brought me close to breaking down altogether.

"What is it?" he repeated.

"Nothing," I managed to reply. "I only wanted to hear the music."

He was looking down at me, smiling and shaking his head a little.

"I'm sorry, Aurion. I should have asked you. Do you want to come in now? He's going to play again in a few minutes."

He had a hand on my shoulder, as if he would propel me through the open door. I resisted.

"No—oh, no! Arax, please. I can't. . . ."

I should have been afraid to join them if I had been invited in the normal way, but to appear late and in this eccentric fashion was more than I could face.

"You don't really care about what those idiots think?" Arax asked.

CHAPTER 11

He still held my shoulder, and I noticed for the first time the dry heat of his touch as he walked me over to the terrace wall.

"Another time . . ." he suggested, and added, "perhaps you're right. We're very Tar-Askan tonight. Two of them," he nodded toward the windows and named two of his companions whom I did not know very well, "have sworn brotherhood today. I thought we should wish them well."

"What does that mean?" I asked, relieved to talk about anything but myself.

"It's a custom—no, it's more serious, or should be. It's a life's commitment. It's finding someone you can trust. Being prepared to give your life for him. Knowing he would do it for you. It's not to be done lightly. Not for—"

He had been speaking with a sincerity that I had never heard in him before. But in the last few words I thought he was beginning to sound angry and he stopped himself as if he realized it too. He looked at me.

"You don't have this custom?"

"No. We might pledge friendship, but this is—"

"This is more. It is a . . . a definite bond." He stumbled a little in his speech as if he were finding words difficult. I had stopped thinking he was drunk, but I could not decide what was wrong with him. "There is a ceremony. It begins with the gift of a knife or a sword. That signifies death. And then they share a cup of wine, and that means life. They have exchanged life and death, and forever after—"

He broke off, gripping the top of the wall.

"Arax, what's the matter?" I cried.

He shook his head as if to clear it.

"Nothing. Nothing, little cousin. Are you sure you won't come in?"

"Yes, quite sure. But Arax—"

"You can't sit out here. It's too cold."

I saw him shiver and I became really alarmed.

"Arax, I think you're ill."

"Ill? Rubbish. I'm never ill. It's this sea breeze. It cuts like a knife. I'm going in." He moved away, and then looked back. "You won't come?"

"No, thank you." He was obviously not going to listen to me. "May I stay and hear the music?"

He waved a hand toward me.

"Help yourself."

Then he was gone, and I retreated toward the top step again. A few moments later two servants appeared. One brought a cloak, the other a cup of wine and a plate of little spiced cakes. They delivered these with their usual impassivity in the face of the peculiarity, if not downright madness, of Tar-Askan lords, and left me. I was warmed by Arax's kindness as much as the cloak, which I did not really need, and almost overcome to think that he had stopped ignoring me. The music began again. I could have been almost entirely happy, except when I remembered Arax's strangeness. I was a healer. I knew there was something wrong. But I also knew there was nothing I could do.

12

The next morning, along with my breakfast, my servant Hithiel brought me the news of the court, as usual. Today he had a particularly interesting item: the lord Arax had collapsed at the end of his party and was in bed with marsh fever. He departed halfway between consternation and excitement, leaving me to my breakfast and my thoughts.

In a way it was a relief. At least now I knew what was wrong. His behavior on the previous night had been disturbing me. The fever was short-lived, although unpleasant. And it might actually do Arax good to realize that even he was not invincible. I went down to practice with my mind at ease, deciding that I dared to visit him and that he would probably be fit to see me by the following day.

So I wasted more than twenty-four hours, for it was the early afternoon of the day after before I went to Arax's rooms. The outer room was empty except for two servants whispering together. An inner door was half open and I caught a movement from behind it. The servants moved toward me as I entered.

"My lord?"

"I have come to see the lord Arax."

They exchanged glances.

"He is ill, my lord."

"I know. That's why I've come to see him."

The second servant interposed, deferentially, but firmly.

"It is not possible at this time, my lord. The priests of Askar are with him."

As if to confirm what he said, a voice from the inner room was raised in a wailing invocation. The sound chilled me, but still I did not understand. I bowed my head.

"Very well. I shall return at a better time."

And so another day was wasted.

It was on the morning of the third day that Hithiel brought the news. He was rather subdued as he laid my breakfast, and announced, "They say the lord Arax will die, my lord."

"Die!" I sprang to my feet, tipping over my chair. Hithiel retrieved it. "What do you mean? No one dies of marsh fever."

He looked shocked.

"But my lord—it is most deadly. . . ."

"Nonsense. You take spearwort root and the leaves—"

I broke off in the face of his evident incomprehension. Then I dismissed him. I had to think.

This was the third day. A marsh fever victim, untreated, might survive for five days if he were strong. And Arax, of course, was strong. But if these people really did not know the simple remedy that we used in the Two Islands, he would die. And I could not imagine him dead. Whenever I thought of Arax, he was in motion—riding, swimming, holding the leopard on his spear. It was absurd to think of his death.

I was drenched in fear, for Arax and for myself, for I knew I must go to the king. He had refused me once. It was quite possible that he would condemn me to death simply for daring to oppose him, or for trying to encroach on the rights of the priests of Askar. A cowardly voice suggested to me that my death would do no one any good—least of all Arax. And that if I died, no one would be left to stop the war with Kerraven. And there were cases of recovery from marsh fever. Not many, but it had happened. I found that I was praying fervently for God to intervene and save Arax.

I was alone in my room, but the very silence seemed to have a body. My prayer was flung back at me. I could almost sense anger. God had brought them together, my skill and Arax's need. It was only my fear that was keeping them apart. I bowed my head into my hands.

"Then please, Lord, give me courage."

That did it. My mind was made up, and I left at once to make my request to see the king.

It was the afternoon before Largh sent for me. I spent the intervening hours in a fury of impatience and desperation. I dared not leave my room before the summons came. I missed practice, but that was trivial. I ignored the midday meal that Hithiel brought. Then after a while I made myself eat a few mouthfuls so that I should have strength for what I had to do.

At last Largh received me in the same reception room. He was seated in the chair with a brooding look. When I went to kneel before him, he stopped me with a movement of the hand.

"Say what you have come to say, and quickly."

I obeyed.

"My lord, your son Arax is ill of the marsh fever. They say he will die."

The king shifted restlessly.

"What of it?"

"My lord, I can cure it."

The great head came up and he looked full into my eyes.

"Ah, yes, the healer. We spoke of this."

"Yes, my lord. And you refused. I accepted that. But now—"

He was waiting, doing nothing to help me.

"My lord, I do not wish to blaspheme against your god. But Arax will die, and he need not! My lord, let me help him. Let me—"

He interrupted me by striking a bell at his side. An inner door opened and a servant entered. For all that I could read in Largh's expression, it might have been an armed guard.

"What would you need to do?" the king asked.

"There is a shrub, my lord—I should need to find it and prepare it, and—"

"How long?"

"By this evening, my lord. By tomorrow we should know."

He snapped his fingers at the servant.

"Go with him. See that he has all he needs."

"Oh, my lord, thank you!"

I turned to go, but he called me back.

"Aurion, when you go to my son you will not find the priests of Askar there. I think it best that you do not meet. And Aurion, if my son should die—"

"If he dies, my lord, you may have my life to use as you see fit."

The king's lips moved into a bleak smile.

"At least you have confidence. In yourself or that strange god of yours. Very well, go."

I hastened down the steps, down toward the main courtyard and the stables, the king's servant only just managing to keep up with me. It was only afterward that I reflected I had not been afraid, only feverishly impatient to gain Largh's consent and start work.

"I need a horse," I said. "First I must find the shrub and pray it grows close by. By the time I get back, I want a room where I can work. And tools—sharp knives, a mortar and pestle, boiling water and clean bowls—everything must be clean."

It never occurred to me that he would disobey, or forget. Tar-Askan servants do neither.

"And find the slave girl, Meriu," I added. "She's quick, and sensible. I want her to help me."

Then I was away on a horse that appeared—saddled and bridled, as if by magic. I remembered where I had seen spearwort growing—near the place I had fallen on the day of the hunt. But fortunately I found it again, much closer, not far from where the road forked. I gathered a huge armful of it, as much as I could stuff into the saddle's leather pouches. Although my concern was for Arax, I knew that I should have more patients soon. There is never only one victim of marsh fever.

When I returned to the palace, Meriu was waiting for me in the courtyard.

"Any news of Arax?" I asked as I slid from the horse.

"He lives."

She had the other news I wanted, too—that what I needed was ready. As she led me away, she asked, "Are you sure you know what you're doing?"

"Yes. Why?"

"It's all around the court that you have pledged your life to save Arax and the king will put you to death if you fail."

I thought about that. I had not seen the situation in quite that way before.

"Is that true?" Meriu asked.

"Yes, I suppose it is."

She sighed exaggeratedly. "Was it really necessary to do it like that?"

"At the time, it seemed inevitable."

There was no reply except a toss of her head. Then a moment later she added, letting her real anxiety show through. "Aurion, are you sure it will be all right?"

That evening, when the spearwort cordial was ready, I took a cup of it to Arax. In the outer room a group of servants were gossiping together. They broke apart, startled at my entry. I crossed to the bedroom. When I opened the door, a cloud of aromatic vapor billowed out to meet me. I could see a brazier with something bubbling on it in a copper bowl. The air was stifling, damp and hot, and the heavy perfume caught at my throat.

"Get rid of that," I ordered the servants who had followed me in. "And open the windows."

They looked shocked, but scurried to obey. I went over to the bed to Arax. He lay still, his breathing shallow, his eyes open, glazed and unrecognizing. His skin was pallid, his hair lifeless and clinging around his face. All the bed coverings were soaked with sweat. I sent the servants for fresh sheets, water, and towels. While I waited, I raised Arax's head and gave him the cordial. At first he resisted and I could not make him understand, but eventually he drank it all. At last I could let myself relax a little. I thought I was in time.

When the servants returned, we bathed Arax, changed the bedding, and settled him more comfortably. The air in the room had cleared. Through the open windows flowed the cool light of evening and a clean breeze from the sea. I dismissed the servants to wait in the outer room and sat beside Arax. I stayed far into the night, bathing his forehead and watching for signs that the fever was abating. Sometimes, even when the fever is gone, a patient will slip into death in spite of anything the healer can do. But I could not believe that of Arax. The spirit in him was too strong and vital.

I must have dozed myself, for the next thing I was aware of was Arax looking at me, his eyes intelligent again, holding a weak trace of their characteristic amusement.

"Little cousin," he murmured.

"Yes."

I suddenly found I was fighting tears, and I turned away to wring out the cloth I was bathing his forehead with. I would have been ashamed to cry in front of him. When I turned back, I had myself in hand again.

"How do you feel?" I asked.

"Like a beached fish," he replied, his voice a faint thread. "That's good, though." He hesitated, frowning slightly, and then went on. "What are you doing here? You'll catch the fever."

"So, I'll catch it."

A flicker of a smile crossed his face. But before he could say more, the door opened and a servant appeared on the threshold.

"My lord Aurion, the king's steward is here and wishes to speak to you."

I looked at Arax, shrugging.

"I'd better go. But I'll come back. You try to sleep."

I left the servant with instructions to stay with him and to call me if necessary, and went out. In the outer room, the king's steward was waiting with Meriu.

"My lord," he began, his alarm and disapproval making an odd mixture with his dignity, "the marsh fever is spreading. The king wishes you to take charge."

"There are three other cases in the court," Meriu added. "And there must be more in the town. I think it's going to be bad, Aurion."

I caught a flicker of surprise from the steward at the way a slave girl saw fit to address me. But I had more important things to think about. I had expected something like this. And in the hours spent with Arax I had given it some thought, so I knew what to ask for now.

"I can't keep moving all over the palace," I said. "I'll be too busy and the infection will spread more quickly that way. I need somewhere to work, separate from the rest of the court and away from the living quarters. My patients will have to come to me. I'll need help, but no one is to be ordered to come, not even slaves. And the king must open the gates so that people from the town can come in. Can you tell him that?"

Even more disapproving, the steward was taking an elaborate leave when I interrupted. "And tell the king also that his son will live."

I smiled, but gently, to see his dignity desert him. He departed almost at a run.

"So your neck should be safe," Meriu commented.

"What? Oh—yes." Somehow I had never been able to take the threat to my life very seriously. "But Meriu, listen. I meant what I said about only accepting help freely given. What about you? Don't feel that you have to take the risk."

"I'm not taking a risk." Her voice was tart, as usual. "I've had the fever already, in Kerraven. And they say that no one ever gets it twice."

"Yes, that's true."

"But what about you, Aurion? Have you had it?"

I shook my head.

"No," I said thoughtfully. "I'm probably going to get it now, though."

For a moment I thought she was going to suggest I keep out of the way. But all she said was, "Then you'd better start teaching me everything I need to know."

This conversation took place in the very early morning. By midday we were installed in our new quarters. The king had assigned to us a courtyard near the main gate known as the Strangers' Court. It was where guests stayed who were not important enough to be lodged with the king. It was just what I wanted, for it was separated from the rest of the palace by a high wall and a single gate.

One large room became my workroom, and we spread mattresses between the columns, where they would be shaded and open to the air. We admitted our patients, now numbering four, and I sent word into the town that anyone sick of the fever could come to us for help. I organized a group of servants to gather spearwort and to bring us food and drink as well as anything else we needed. They were to leave everything outside the gate. Only those willing to risk the fever would enter the Strangers' Court.

Among these was my servant Hithiel. I felt ashamed, for I had written him off as an amiable little gossip, and I had not expected to see him there. I set him to pounding spearwort root. I returned sometime later to find him in the grip of the fever, trying to support himself against the table and continue with his task. The fever had struck him quickly, as it sometimes does. I had seen none of the signs on him when he came in.

Gently I took the mortar and pestle away from him, and asked, "Why didn't you tell me you were feeling ill?"

"I wanted to help you, my lord. Not—not be a nuisance. . . ."

His voice broke in a terrified sob. I half carried him to a mattress and knelt beside him.

"Listen, Hithiel, you're not going to die. I promise you. The next day or two will be bad, but you will be all right."

He was managing to control himself, half believing me, frightened eyes locked onto my face. I realized Meriu was beside me with a cup of the cordial. I thanked her and steadied it for Hithiel while he drank.

"That's right," I said. "Now lie down and try to rest. And don't be afraid."

As soon as I saw that he was settled, I left him and moved along the columns to Meriu, who was waiting for me outside the workroom. Her face was pink from standing over the fires that were heating water. She brushed wisps of hair back from her face.

"We need more spearwort," she said.

"There's a party out now. They should be back soon. There's plenty of it up in the hills. Anything else?"

"If we had some reed mats, we could hang them between the columns, for more shade."

"Good idea. I'll send for some."

"And I think you should go and get some sleep."

I started to protest, but she would not listen.

"Nothing is happening now that I can't cope with. I've put a mattress in that little room at the end. Go in there, and I'll call you when I need you."

She gave me a little push.

"Go on, Aurion. I didn't sit up all night with Arax, remember? And you're the one who's at risk. Don't tell me you can go on indefinitely without sleep."

There was obviously no arguing with her in this mood. And she was right. I must take the chance to sleep while I could. My last conscious thoughts were of feeling grateful to her.

14

I slept until late afternoon, when Meriu called me to check on our patients and to eat a meal she had prepared. Three more fever victims had come in, all from the town. Meriu had given them the spearwort cordial, and for the moment there was nothing more to be done. I was pleased that the townspeople had heard they could get help at the palace and were prepared to come. Along with the others, I visited Hithiel, who was now deep in the power of the fever. Though I sat beside him for a while, he was not aware of me.

The new batch of spearwort had come in and Meriu had already begun to prepare it. I helped her, only interrupted from time to time by the arrival of new patients. When the cordial was ready, I took a cup of it and went to visit Arax.

As I was entering the outer room, there was a crash, and a servant shot out from the bedroom.

"What's the matter?" I asked.

"My lord Arax," he gasped. "He threw a cup at me. And told me to bring him some food and wine."

"Do nothing of the sort," I told him.

I went in, retrieved the cup from the floor near the door, and crossed over to Arax who was in bed, propped up by pillows.

"You aren't strong enough yet to be exerting yourself, my lord," I said. I handed him the cordial. "For the moment you may have that, and you—" I turned to the servant, who had followed me in cautiously—"may bring some fruit juice. Tomorrow, some milk or broth. No solid food of any kind until the day after."

The servant looked blank. I had half expected Arax to

explode, but instead his face was lit with amusement. He waved a hand at the servant.

"Go. Do it."

When the servant had gone, Arax patted the bed for me to sit down. He sipped experimentally at the cup of cordial I had given him.

"Foul brew," he muttered.

"Drink it," I said, and added, "if you please, my lord."

He grinned at me.

"You're getting above yourself, little cousin."

Then his voice and expression suddenly changed.

"They tell me you gave me my life." When I said nothing, he went on, unable to keep the mischief out of his voice for long. "That sort of thing is beginning to be a habit—one that I hope you will cultivate."

"Of course, my lord."

Somehow we were at ease together. I was glad to see him getting well. He was already regaining his strength. Of course, not even marsh fever could subdue Arax for long. I knew I should go back to my work in the Strangers' Court, but I did not want to leave. It was not often that I had had his companionship without some trouble to disturb it. At least, I thought, I would stay until the servant returned.

Arax was drinking the cordial with an expression of distaste. I was watching him, not feeling the need to talk, when he asked me curiously, "Did you call on your god to save my life?"

The question took me off balance. I was not sure how to answer it, or even exactly what he meant.

"In a way—" I was beginning, when he interrupted.

"The priests called on Askar, but the servants tell me he did nothing."

There was something very wrong about that. Without suspecting it, I had been thrust on to a point of decision. Could I tell him my God had healed him when Askar was powerless and win his allegiance with a lie? And yet there was a sense in which it would not be a lie. I tried to choose words carefully.

"Arax, my God did not heal you by a miracle. That foul brew

you're drinking is a cure for the marsh fever, and we know it well in the Two Islands. That is what healed you. But I believe my God gave me my skill, and I thank Him for it. And Arax—your father had already forbidden me to use the craft of healing. I was afraid to make him angry by asking again. If I had not prayed to my God for courage, I might never have dared to face him a second time."

Arax was looking interested.

"So you faced my father?" he asked. "Well, heads have come off for less. I can see your point, Aurion, but if you ask me, your god goes a strange way to work."

"That is His way," I said, hardly daring to believe that he was taking me seriously. "We are His hands to use in the world."

Arax nodded.

"I'll think of it," he said, finishing the cordial and handing me the cup with an expression of relief. "It is not Askar's way."

"It might be a better way."

He made no comment, and I did not feel that I could push him any further.

This time when I returned to the Strangers' Court I meant to stay there until the outbreak of fever was over. I had no more fears about Arax. My place now was with the others who needed me. By the end of that day, the number of victims had risen to sixteen, and I knew that was only the beginning.

In the end, I lost count of the days. Meriu told me afterwards that it was almost three weeks from the first case of fever to the last. In that time we cared for more than a hundred people from the palace and the town. At one point there were over forty of them lying between the columns. Of the hundred, only three died. Two of those were very old, and the third, from one of the outlying farms, came to us too late.

I thought, too, that we would lose Hithiel. Toward the end of the second day, I despaired of the fever's breaking. I made him drink more of the cordial, but nothing seemed to have any effect. I felt he was slipping away from me, when I had only just begun to know him. I could not forget that I had promised him he would not die.

Then the fever left him almost as swiftly as it had come. I had been attending some of the others, and when I returned he lay so quiet that I feared he was dead. But as I knelt beside him he turned to look at me.

"Your god must be very powerful, my lord," he whispered.

I tried to explain to him, as I had tried to explain to Arax, but I doubt he understood. He only smiled at me and settled contentedly into sleep. I was anxious about him for a day or so afterward, but he regained strength quickly, and his old cheerfulness with it.

Most of my patients, when they began to recover, left us and went to be cared for by their families. But Hithiel had no one, so he stayed with us. As soon as he could sit up, Meriu found him some light task to do, which he carried out with great care, happy to be of use at last.

Nothing of course, could have happened without Meriu. She seemed untiring. Neither of us had much time for sleep, but she was always fresh and brisk, with the caustic tongue that hid her kindness and her faith, but did not hide them very effectively from me or from anyone under her care in the Strangers' Court.

At last we realized that fewer new cases were coming in. The number of our patients dropped. Some of the earliest victims, now recovered and immune from the disease, came back to help us. At last there was a little time to rest. I had been sleeping in the end room which Meriu and I shared—since one of us was always awake and on duty—and I woke to realize it was evening. When I went into the workroom, Meriu was lighting the lamps. To my eyes the flames seemed blurred and yet glaring, and they hurt my eyes. My mouth was parched. I went to pour a cup of water. The jug felt heavy. I splashed water over my hands and the table, and knocked over the cup.

Meriu turned at the sound.

"Aurion, what in the world are you—"

She broke off and came over to me. I could not make my eyes focus on her face, and her voice sounded remote, pulsing loud and soft. She put a hand to my forehead, and then pressed me back into a chair.

CHAPTER 14

"Hmm. I know what's the matter with you."

She went away to return a moment later and thrust a cup into my hands. It was not until I tasted the bitter cordial that I understood.

"No!" I protested. "It isn't that. I'm tired, that's all." I shook my head to try to clear it. "I'll be all right in a minute."

"You'll be all right in about two days, if you drink that," Meriu said.

A wave of shivering swept over me. I would have dropped the cup if Meriu had not caught hold of it.

"Drink it," she insisted.

"But I can't . . . there's too much to do—"

"Rubbish. Drink it and stop arguing."

I was too tired and felt too ill to go on resisting. I drank the cordial, understanding at last why Arax had called it a foul brew.

"Now go back to bed," Meriu said.

I got up and took a step. The lamps reeled and twisted in a mad dance. I reached the door. I remember clutching the door post. Then all consciousness left me and I went down into the roaring dark.

15

The first sensation I was aware of was a delicious coolness on my forehead and the scent of sweet herbs. I was lying in bed and I wondered what I was doing there. Someone was sitting beside me.

"Meriu?" I asked.

I opened my eyes. It was Arax, bathing my forehead. I was in my own bed in my own room. The very faint light of early morning was filtering through the windows. At once I remembered that I should have been in the Strangers' Court. I tried to sit up, but I found that I was too weak. Arax laid a hand on my shoulder.

"Lie still."

Briefly I went on struggling, but it was hopeless.

"I can't stay here. There's work to be done. Meriu—"

"Meriu, if that's her name, is managing very nicely."

"But she can't—not alone. She needs help."

Arax gave an exasperated sigh.

"Aurion, she isn't alone. She has all the help she needs. Relax."

I had to give in. Already the effort had exhausted me. When he saw that I was quiet, Arax smiled and went on.

"She came to see you not long ago and gave me a message for you. There were only two new cases after you and none at all for the last two days. It's over, Aurion."

"None at all for—then how long have I been here?"

"Four days."

"Four—but the fever only lasts for two."

Arax grinned.

"You would have to be different."

I lay back, too tired to take it all in. I was only beginning to understand that the outbreak was at an end. Arax went on bathing my forehead. Something about that disturbed me and I put up a hand to stop him.

"Don't, my lord."

He brushed away my hand as if it were a troublesome insect.

"Why not?"

"It isn't fitting."

"You did it for me."

I sighed.

"That was different."

"Rubbish."

I closed my eyes, suddenly overwhelmed by his presence there, and my anxiety about Meriu and the duties I should be carrying out. I began to understand why it is that some fever victims die after the fever has left them. I felt as if I lay at the bottom of a black pit. I knew I could climb out of it, back to light and life, but I could not summon the strength even to begin. It would be easier to let the darkness take me.

It was not until Arax said, "Aurion, what is it?" that I realized I was weeping.

I turned my head away from him.

"Nothing. I don't know."

A moment later I felt him take my hands.

"Aurion, listen. You've done wonders. Everyone thinks so, except possibly the priests of Askar. And they can't do anything while my father favors you. Dozens of people have been here, asking after you. They've been coming up from the town with presents. You'll see, Aurion, when you're well again. Everyone will honor you."

I heard him, but the words meant nothing and I could not stop the tears. That was not what I had intended. In my real task I had failed utterly.

"I don't want it," I said. "I want to go home."

There was silence for a moment, and then Arax spoke quietly.

"Aurion, there's nothing I can do now. But later, when I'm king, you shall go back to the Two Islands. And you shall be king after your father. I know it isn't much, it's so far ahead, but isn't it something to hope for?"

I turned back toward him. He was looking down at me gravely. For the first time since I had known him he seemed unsure of himself. I wanted to say something. Not just to thank him, but to show him what it meant to me, that he should take thought for me. But between weakness and despair, no words would come. I felt darkness gathering around me again, heard his voice, strong and reassuring, and then nothing.

Later I woke again. This time I was alone. Black despair still followed me, but now I had to face it. I had failed. I had been given my chance and lost it. If I had claimed that the power of my God had cured the marsh fever by a miracle when I called on Him, then by now a great wave of belief in the true God would have been sweeping over Tar-Askar. The power of Askar would have been broken. The war would have been stopped. Instead, the honor was being paid to me, and I did not want it.

For the time being I had forgotten that I had tried to explain what I thought God's real part had been, and how I could have done nothing without Him. I felt that I had thrown away the only hope of bringing Tar-Askar to the true God.

While these thoughts were going around in my head, Hithiel came in.

"Oh, my lord, I'm sorry! I just went out into the courtyard for a few minutes, for these."

He showed me a handful of flowers, poured some water into a cup and set them where I could see them. Somehow the tiny act of kindness made me feel better. I said to Hithiel, "Bring me another pillow. I want to sit up."

He obeyed at once, and brought me some fruit juice to drink. He was obviously delighted that I was getting well and that he could fuss over me. I looked him over carefully. He still seemed frail from the fever, but it would have been cruel to scold him for going back to his duties.

"Are you well now, Hithiel?" I asked.

"Oh, yes, my lord, thank you!" He came to the bedside and knelt swiftly. There were tears in his eyes. "I owe it all to you, my lord."

For a moment he hesitated, his finger tracing a thread in the embroidered bed cover. Then he asked me, "My lord—not now, but later, when you're stronger—would you tell me more about your God?"

He scarcely waited for my assent before he went on, the words spilling out of him now that he had made a beginning.

"I know your God saved me. I don't understand how, but I might if you explained it to me. And the worship of Askar—it frightens me, my lord! I'm only a servant, I'll never be a warrior. And anyway, I don't want to be, I'm not brave enough. All Askar ever teaches us is to fight and kill and look for power. I don't want that, any of it!"

He drew back, looking half ashamed of his outburst, but determined to go on to the end of what he had to say.

"I've heard them saying that your God teaches peace. I've heard some of the young lords, laughing about it. They said that a God like that would deserve to be put to death, but I—I don't understand. But I want to, if you would teach me, my lord."

"Yes, Hithiel. Yes, of course I will."

If I had been myself, I should have rejoiced to hear him. But down in the depths of my black pit a voice sneered at me.

"He is only one, after all. And no more than a servant. How will he ever help you to stop the war?"

And I had no strength left in me to find a reply.

16

I did not see Meriu in the next few days. Hithiel told me she came once to see me when I was asleep. She was busy in the Strangers' Court, caring for the last few patients, and I did not want to drag her away. But for all that, I needed her. If I had spoken to her, I would have shared my thoughts with her. I do not think my black depression would have survived her sharp common sense. And in that case, what next took place would probably never have happened at all.

Arax, too, stayed away until three days later, when he strode unannounced into my room and demanded to know how I was feeling.

"Much better, my lord, thank you," I replied. "I thought I might get up later."

For some reason he frowned.

"I don't think you should. Listen, Aurion . . ."

He glanced across the room to where Hithiel was busy with something in the far corner. He seemed to decide that he would not interfere, and sat beside me on the bed.

"Aurion, tomorrow is the Autumn Festival."

That meant absolutely nothing to me. I was aware of a sudden movement from Hithiel, but when I looked at him he was turned away from me, fussing with the folds of one of my tunics.

"It is one of the great festivals of Askar," Arax went on. "Twice a year, all the young men of the court and the town stand before the priests in the courtyard of the temple. The god chooses one of them to be sent to him."

I did not understand.

"Sent to him?"

"On the following day the high priest will put him to death and his spirit will go to join the god."

For a moment I stared at him, saying nothing. Then everything I had heard about Askar's cruelty came rushing back into my mind. Of course it fit, but even then I found it hard to believe.

"You sacrifice to the god?" I asked.

"We offer him the best we have."

There was a kind of pride in the way Arax spoke. He was completely serious, which was unusual for him. It was that, more than anything else, which brought home to me the gravity of what he was saying.

"And why have you come to tell me?" I asked him.

He leaned forward and clasped my hand.

"Aurion, I said all the young men of the court. You would be expected to go, too."

I sat erect.

"But I—"

"I know. You serve a different god. That would not make any difference. But what I'm trying to tell you—if anyone is ill, he need not go. That would be asking the god to accept imperfection. So stay here, Aurion, don't try to get up, for the next day or two at least. Wait until it's all over."

I lay back against my pillows, too shocked to think. It was not fear—though even then I realized that there would be other festivals, when I would have no excuse to stay away—but more like outrage that any god could claim allegiance who demanded such a barbaric price from his worshipers.

"And do you go?" I asked Arax. "You're the king's son. Surely you—"

He interrupted me, rising to his feet.

"Yes, I stand before the priests," he said. "Aurion, one day I shall be king. Could I ask my people to do something that I would not do myself?"

Now the pride was plain to see. His head was lifted and there was a light in his eyes. His passing interest in my God had faded before the exultation of offering himself as a sacrifice for his people.

Then I heard a definite sound from Hithiel's corner—the sound of a stifled sob.

"Hithiel—you too?"

He came to me then, on his knees by the bed, his hand reaching blindly for mine. He was shaking with terror. Arax looked down at him pityingly, as if considering how unlikely it was that the god would ever choose such a pathetic little creature.

"Oh, my lord, pray to your God for me," Hithiel begged. "Pray that I won't be chosen. No." He went on before I had the chance to reply. "No, that would be be wrong. Someone must be chosen. Please pray for courage for me."

I assured him that I would, and slowly he began to recover his self-control. He begged forgiveness from me and from Arax for his lapse from dutiful silence. Arax waved him away impatiently, his attention still on me.

"You'll stay away tomorrow?" he asked.

Something inside me told that I should go and stand with them. But I could see how stupid that would be. Arax would not thank me for it, and Hithiel would be ashamed to have brought me into danger. Despair seemed to close its hand more tightly around me. There was nothing I could do.

"Yes, I'll stay away," I promised.

I asked Hithiel to wake me early the next morning, and he did so. My windows showed as faint gray squares and the room was still half shrouded in darkness. Hithiel was rigidly calm.

"I've put out a fresh tunic, my lord, in case you want to get up. And your breakfast is on the table. Do you want anything else?"

"No, Hithiel, thank you. Come straight back when it's over."

"Yes, my lord, I will, if—" His voice broke. "Pray for me," he whispered and darted away.

When he had gone, I could not stay in bed. I got up at once, feeling shaky, but pleased that my strength was returning. I splashed my hands and face in water that Hithiel had left ready. I dressed and looked at my breakfast, but the thought of it turned me sick. I could not get out of my mind what would be happening when the sun rose in the courtyard of the temple of Askar. I tried to give my mind to prayer, but my fears and my disgust were so great that I could not form coherent words. In the end I could only lay what I felt before God and leave it in His hands.

That should have been enough, but it was not. As the minutes went by, I was consumed by a mounting terror for Arax. Not for Hithiel. In my heart I knew he would be safe. But for Arax—for if a god were truly to choose the best and the most brilliant as his sacrifice, who else would he choose but Arax? It made no difference that there was no god to speak. I could not suppress my fear.

I could not stay in the room. Moving around had strengthened me. At least I could not distinguish any longer between weakness from the fever and the effects of growing terror. I had to get out. The Fountain Court was still gray and netted with cobwebs. The cadence of water was all that broke the silence. I passed through it. I remembered in my explorations coming upon a terrace from which I could see a section of the temple courtyard, further down the hill. That was where I was headed. If I could not intervene, at least I could see.

The morning light was growing as I reached it. Crouched on a step in the wall, I was concealed from all but the closest scrutiny from below. I could see the front of the temple with great bronze doors that now stood open. They were guarded by scarlet-plumed spearmen. A flight of steps led up to them. At the top, before the doors, King Largh sat in a carved chair. He was robed in gold with a great jeweled headdress and a scepter across his knees. The priests—five of them, scarlet-cloaked—stood around him. A sixth bent over a copper dish that held blazing coals. The smoke was whipped away by a breeze into the morning sky. Further away, beneath the temple walls, stood a row of trumpeters, their instruments lowered.

The body of the courtyard at the foot of the steps was crowded. I could not see all of it from where I sat. It was difficult to pick out individuals. I looked in vain for Hithiel, but Arax I saw in the first glance. No one could mistake the height or the bright golden hair or the confidence with which he held himself. He stood close to the steps, not far away from his father. I marveled that Largh could let his only son take such a risk. I doubted for a moment that the king's son would ever be chosen, whatever he himself might believe. But it was not enough to allay my fear.

My heart was pounding. I wanted to look away, but my eyes were fixed on the scene. Everything in the courtyard was still. Then the blazing rim of the sun crept above the palace buildings. The trumpets flashed as they rose in a single arc. Their notes brayed out and were silent. Into the silence came a voice from the priest who stood with his arms raised before the fire, a voice crying out a single word, a single name. I could not hear what it was, but it was followed by a stir in the courtyard, and the sound of distant screaming.

I sat with my eyes closed, sick and shaking. I had meant to slip away before anyone discovered me, but I could not have moved if discovery had brought my death. Presently I heard the sound of footsteps, murmured conversation, an occasional burst of laughter. I realized that the assembly had broken up. I must get back to my room. With untold effort I opened my eyes and saw Arax standing in front of me.

He had been grim the day before, proud and unapproachable. Now he had recovered his old, teasing smile.

"Little cousin!" he said. "Watching our ceremony?" He leaned forward and took my hands. "You're ice cold. You would have been better in bed."

"Who—" I whispered.

He spoke a name I did not know. I found that I was clinging to him, not able to express my fears, not really wanting him to know, but betrayed by my own lack of control. I became aware of two or three of the others standing behind him, Idric for one, and of the looks of mockery I was attracting. I began to feel ashamed of myself.

"I'm sorry," I said. "I didn't mean—"

"It's all right." This time, as often before, his teasing was shot through with gentleness. "Shall I take you back to your room?"

"Oh no, my lord. I'll go now . . . please don't—"

Again he interrupted my babbling.

"Shall I see you tonight? I'm giving a party, for the Festival. Will you come?"

I tried to draw back, but he kept a grip on my hands.

"Oh no, my lord, I can't—"

He grinned mischievously.

"Come on, little cousin, just for once. There'll be music. And I'll send you something decent to wear. No—" forestalling my protest—"don't be so prickly. Everyone gives presents at Festival."

And something, whether it was his smile, the whispers of the others, or the sudden relaxing of tension, drove me into what proved to be the final indiscretion.

"Yes, all right, my lord. Thank you. I'll come."

17

I slept for part of the day and woke in time to get ready for Arax's celebration. Thinking it over, I was sure it was a mistake. I had no right to be participating, in however small a way, in the festival of Askar. And I knew that few people there, apart from Arax himself, would be pleased to see me. But I had given my word and I could not back out now.

Hithiel had recovered from the morning's ordeal, with a stirring of pride in himself because he had not given way to fear. He was naïvely excited when I told him I was to go to Arax's party, and anxious that I should look my best. I let him attend to my bath and wash and cut my hair, which he did expertly. Toward evening, one of Arax's servants delivered a tunic for me to wear.

I had not forgotten about that. I had been feeling rather nervous, remembering some of the elaborate clothes that the Tar-Askan lords favored. Whatever it was like, I should have to wear it. When it arrived, I was relieved. The tunic was of dark blue silk, severely plain. It was rich enough for a king's son, but unlikely to draw attention to me. I put it on and could not help feeling faintly pleased as I looked at my reflection in the polished mirror.

That was not, however, the end of my anxiety. I remembered Arax's words, "Everyone gives presents at Festival." He had been generous to me, and he was my host. I ought to give something to him, but I had so little that was suitable, and no money or time to buy anything. I was still undecided when it was time to go. I had already dismissed Hithiel. I tried to tell myself it did not matter, but I was determined not to go without a gift. At last

I settled on my hunting knife. The craftsmanship was the finest in the Two Islands, and it was something that Arax might appreciate and use. Hastily catching it up, I went out.

My hesitation had made me late. When I arrived on the terrace outside Arax's rooms where I had once sat and listened to the musician, the windows already blazed with light. I could hear voices, laughter, and a thread of music running through it all. I paused. I had an impulse to turn away. Perhaps I had met with greater dangers, but never anything more difficult than stepping through that door in the midst of Arax's friends.

At first I could not see him, but one or two of the others greeted me in a more friendly way than before. Then I recognized someone who had been my patient in the Strangers' Court. He came up and thanked me and asked if I were recovering now. We talked a little about Meriu. Gradually I began to feel more at ease.

Then Arax appeared, thrusting through the crowd in high spirits. He was pleased to see me. He admired the tunic and called a servant to bring wine.

"Arax," I interrupted, "you told me that everyone gives presents at Festival. I brought you this."

I held out the hunting knife. There was a sudden silence. Arax stared at it as if he had never seen one before. I realized something was wrong, but as yet I did not understand. Everyone's attention was on us. My friend from the Strangers' Court had retreated a pace or two, looking highly embarrassed.

"Arax—" I began, but my voice failed.

He said nothing, but he looked up at me from the knife, his eyes very bright and intent. Then I heard Idric's voice and saw him in the crowd, his face alive with malice.

"He would like to swear brotherhood with you, Arax," he drawled. Every word showed how much he was enjoying himself. "Aren't you going to answer him?"

Then I remembered. That night on the terrace, Arax had told me about the brotherhood ceremony and how it was a lifetime bond—a trust between two people that would hold until death. He had told me that the ceremony began with the gift of a knife. So much had happened since then, and it had not seemed to have very much to do with me, that I had forgotten completely, until now.

Someone uncomfortably said, "He didn't know—" but Idric interrupted.

"He thinks he is as good as Tar-Askans. Just because of the fever cure—grubbing for roots like a slave—he thinks he's fit to be your brother."

And Torac's voice, though I could not see him, added, "Arax, none of us would dare. . . ."

Idric pushed forward and grasped Arax's shoulder.

"Aren't you going to tell him—"

All this while Arax had not moved or spoken, but went on looking at me with that bright, expectant gaze. He took no more notice of Idric than of a fly alighting on his shoulder. But I remembered the leopard hunt, how he had looked at me and spoken then, the soft voice and the cutting words, "Aurion, no one disgraces me twice."

I let the knife fall and fled.

Behind me I heard a burst of laughter, and I thought—but I was not sure—that Arax called my name. I ignored it. I ran down the steps, down, not thinking where I was going, only that I had to get away. All around me were lighted windows and the sounds of music and laughter, as if everyone were celebrating Festival. I met no one. I was terrified that the others might follow me and find me. I doubled back between buildings and across terraces, but always going down. At the head of one flight of steps I stumbled and fell, half stunned, but I got up and went on. At last I came to the gate that led out on to the beach.

No one was there. I stood, gasping for breath, and looked out across the bay. I knew what I was going to do. I slid out of my sandals, unfastened my tunic, and let it fall. I walked out into the sea. I remembered Arax's words. "To the left of the rock, a current sets out to sea. That's the last anyone would see of you. . . ."

I could not go back to the palace. It was not the mockery of Arax's friends; I had faced that before. And I could have survived Arax's anger, but my mistake had shown me something that I had not dared to admit, even to myself. I could never have asked Arax to be my brother, but that was what I wanted. Meriu had seen it from the beginning. He was important to me. I would have given my life for him, willingly. But I was nothing to him. Only his "little cousin," to be teased, protected if need be, tossed a kind word now and again, as carelessly as he would have treated his horse or his dogs. I could not go on knowing that.

I was ice-cold, and the water felt warm. I swam out slowly. Somewhere at the back of my mind I knew that what I was doing was wrong. All I had ever been taught told me that. I knew that I should face what I had done, go back and take up the task my father had laid on me. But I could not. I had fought, and lost. It was too difficult. I felt the tug of the current and let myself drift with it. That was easy. And in a little while, nothing would matter anymore.

18

I felt as if I had been drifting for hours, though it was not, I suppose, very long. There was nothing except the soft lap of the sea. Above my head shone bright moonlight turning all to silver, and a scattering of stars. Gradually I became aware that my peace was being disturbed. A voice was calling my name. How that could be I did not know.

I turned. I could see the dark head of another swimmer, cutting through the water a few yards away. My mind screamed a silent protest. I kicked out, away from him. Then I realized the futility of that and waited for him to come up to me. I knew from the first it was Arax.

This time there was nothing quiet about his fury. He was shouting at me before he reached my side.

"Aurion—what do you think you're doing? You're in the current! You can't get back!"

"I know. I don't want to get back." Then, like a cold weight descending on me, I understood. Arax could not get back either. In something approaching panic, I cried out, "Why didn't you leave me alone?"

"Leave you? I don't want you dead."

"You're angry with me."

I never thought then how strange it was that we should be confronting each other in the middle of the sea, with death ready to take both of us.

"Of course I'm angry! Of all the stupid, senseless, unnecessary . . . Do you really care what those idiots think about you?"

His onslaught bewildered me. I realized that he had risked

his life for me. I meant something to him after all. And if that were true, I did not want to die. I saw what I had done, and with the knowledge came fear.

"Arax, I'm sorry—I didn't . . . Arax, what can we do?"

"Don't panic, to begin with." His voice was suddenly strong. The anger vanished. "The fishing fleet will pick us up. Just hope that they aren't too far out."

"How far—?"

"Relax. Don't waste your strength. The current will take us."

So we drifted again, side by side. But the peaceful night had turned to horror. I tried to control my breathing, remembering for the first time that I had been ill. My strength was ebbing. I knew that if I died I would have thrown Arax's life away too.

"How did you find me?" I asked.

"I was looking for you. I saw a swimmer out here from the walls and your clothes on the beach. Idiot . . ."

His voice died away.

"What is it?"

"I saw . . . from the walls . . ." The look on his face terrified me. "Aurion, it's Festival night. The fishing boats don't go out."

I followed his gaze. We were approaching the open sea. Before us was a shining, flat surface, broken by a gentle swell. There was no sign of the dark shape of a boat, or the tiny lights that burned at their prows—nothing but the rocky line of the promontory that marked the entrance to the bay.

I felt Arax's hand grasp my shoulder briefly.

"Aurion, there's one chance. Swim across the current. We might make the point."

He struck out at once and I followed. The shore looked quite close. But the current, bearing us along, was strong. Now I was tiring—not the good tiredness at the end of a long swim, but a leaden exhaustion that weighed down my limbs. I could not remember a time when I was not at home in the water. But now I learned how a poor swimmer must feel, out of his depth and out of reach of the shore. Every stroke was an untold effort, and I would have given up, but for Arax at my side.

"Go on," I gasped. "Don't stay with me. You could get help . . . a boat—"

"You'd never last," he replied grimly, still keeping pace with me. "Besides, it's no use. Look."

The last rocks of the point were slipping past us, as the current swept us out to sea. Looking back I could see the whole curve of the bay. Along it were the lights of the town and the palace, and dark against the sky the wooded hills where we had hunted. It was as if all my life in Tar-Askar was gliding away from me. Then a wave surged over me, and I went under.

I seemed to sink forever, struggling helplessly, without the strength to fight my way back to the surface. Desperate for air, I gulped in water. A spinning darkness was engulfing me.

Then I resurfaced, thrashing and coughing water. I heard Arax's voice, urgently, beside me. "Aurion—here. Hold on. Don't—"

I cried out something. For a few minutes I was half out of my mind with fear and remorse because I had led him into this. I tried to plunge away from him, wanting to die so that he would be free to save himself. He grappled with me briefly, shouting something I did not hear. Then he raised his hand and struck me sharply across the face.

That quieted me. I heard my own voice, half sobbing.

"Arax—don't . . ."

He seemed to understand.

"I'm not going to leave you." It was that voice I knew well, soft and charged with anger. "And even alone, I couldn't swim back against the current. We're together. I'm not giving up, either. Just do as you're told, that's all."

I nodded, tried to reply, and choked on a mouthful of water. The struggle had taken the last of my strength. Now it was all I could do to keep afloat. Arax moved closer to me.

"Put your hands on my shoulders. That's right. Rest. And for Askar's sake, be quiet. I'm trying to think."

Now I could do nothing but obey him. We drifted silently. The shore grew more distant, and I caught only glimpses of the palace lights when a wave lifted us. After a while I had to speak.

"Arax, I'm sorry."

Surprisingly, he grinned at me.

"Don't make a habit of it, little cousin." After a pause he added, "I'm trying to remember the currents and tides. If we can last until morning the tide might bring us in, farther along the coast. It's possible."

He grinned at me again. "All the same, if that god of yours answers prayers, you might see if he's listening."

I was too ashamed to pray for myself, but I could, and did, for Arax. I was seeing what had called to me in him—the courage and strength, the invincible spirit, and the essential goodness that would not let him abandon me. I professed to serve a God higher than Askar, but it was Arax who had behaved like God's true servant. And nothing I had done had brought him any closer to belief. That was a failure worse than all the rest.

I was distracted from these thoughts by his voice, suddenly changed.

"Aurion!"

"What is it?"

"I think . . . over there—a light."

I turned my head to follow his gesture. At first I saw nothing but the glittering curve of a wave. Then as we rose to its crest I did see a faint flicker of light, gone almost at once as the next wave swelled up between.

"Is it on shore?" I asked.

"There's nothing over there. It must be a boat. And not far, or we wouldn't see it at all."

We strained to see through the darkness and the surge of the sea. At first I feared we had both imagined it. But then we saw it again and again, in much the same place. And though it was hard to be sure, there was the darker shape of a boat's hull.

"A boat! It must be!" Arax said.

Still supporting me, he struck out in the direction of the light.

"I feel better. I think I could swim," I said.

"Try, then."

Even at that point he could take thought for my self-respect and understand that I did not want to be dragged on board like a drowning kitten. He stayed beside me. And now that I had rested and mastered my panic, I was able to swim again, though I felt slow and clumsy.

Soon the boat took definite shape in front of us. Arax raised an arm and shouted. There was an answering cry, but the boat did not move. Its sails were down. It looked like a fishing boat at anchor. Though I felt at every stroke that I would have to ask Arax for help again, we were drawing close to the boat. Arax swam ahead, caught hold of the side and held out a hand to me. I grasped it and he drew me in.

The occupant of the boat looked over at us and a tart voice said, "The things you men get up to at Festival!"

The shock almost made me lose my hold. It was Meriu.

19

Meriu reached down and helped me over the side. I collapsed, shivering, in the bottom of the boat. I felt it lurch as Arax climbed aboard. Crisply, he said, "Have you a cloak, girl?"

She handed him a bundle which he shook out and wrapped around me. Barely conscious, I clutched the rough wool thankfully and leaned against Arax.

"And what in Askar's name are you doing out here?" Arax went on in the same imperious way.

"In Askar's name, nothing." Meriu replied. "Apart from that, fishing."

I had never seen them together before, but I remembered Arax had seen her while I lay ill with the fever. He seemed taken aback to be spoken to like that by a slave girl.

"No one fishes on a festival night," he said.

Meriu gave an exaggerated sigh.

"The festival is for men and followers of Askar." She spoke as she might have addressed a child who was slow to learn his lesson. "I am not a man nor a follower of Askar. So I'm fishing. It's just as well for you that I am."

Arax was looking disapproving as he listened to this. As she finished, he said, "That's all very well, but you'll have to take us back now. My lord Aurion needs to rest."

Meriu gave him a cold look. "I haven't caught enough yet."

"Are you arguing with me, girl?"

I tried to sit up, and caught at the hand that restrained me. "Don't, Arax. It doesn't matter. I'm all right."

"It won't take much longer," Meriu assured him, "especially if you help."

Arax looked outraged. Then suddenly he threw back his head and laughed.

"I'll say one thing, I've never spent a Festival night like this before. And I'm not sure I don't prefer it to drinking with that crowd of fools back there. All right, girl, show me which rope to pull."

He looked down at me, his amusement fading.

"Are you sure you're all right?"

I nodded. Already another black tide was closing over my head and I let myself slip back into it. I was exhausted, but my sleep was troubled. More than once I jerked half-awake, enough to know where I was. Then I slid into unconsciousness once more.

When I woke fully, I heard Arax and Meriu talking. They were in the midst of an argument. Arax was saying, "But I stood before the priests of Askar and offered him my life."

"No," Meriu replied, "you offered him your death. It takes a lot more effort to offer your life to anything. You haven't even started."

Arax began to reply, not sounding offended. But then he noticed that I was awake, and bent over me, asking how I felt. I reassured him, but I soon slept again, so I never knew if they resolved their argument.

This time my sleep was deeper. When I woke again, feeling stiff and thirsty, the sky was light. The boat was running before a stiff breeze. I sat up and saw that we were already approaching the stretch of beach where the rest of the fishing boats were moored. Arax was steering. In the prow Meriu was bending over her reed baskets that were filled with silver fish.

Arax nodded and smiled at me.

"Home for breakfast soon," he promised.

At the sound of his voice, Meriu turned to look at me.

"Oh, you're awake, are you?"

"Was it a good catch?" I asked.

"Good enough."

It occurred to me to wonder what she was doing there. After the first shock, I had been too exhausted to care.

"Why were you out fishing, Meriu?" I asked. "That can't be one of your tasks."

"No, it's not. But the fisherman—the one this boat belongs to—is hurt. His wife told me a knife slipped, but I think he was in a fight. His arm and his face are slashed, and the cuts look infected."

"You should have told me!"

"I only just found out myself. He can't do his job, and his wife and children are starving. I thought the first thing to do was take the boat out. They'll have food now and the rest of the catch to sell. I'm a fisherman's daughter myself, don't forget."

She turned away from me to look ahead, for we were drawing close to the beach.

"Can you bring her in without wrecking her?" she asked Arax carelessly over one shoulder.

Clearly they had come to some arrangement during the night, for Arax only grinned and said, "Watch me."

He slid neatly between two other boats. Meriu leapt down into the water and guided the boat up on to the beach. Arax stretched and relaxed.

"Breakfast," he said.

"There's work to do first," Meriu snapped. "Hand me down those baskets."

To my surprise he obeyed with no more than an expressive glance at me. I was still too shaky to be much help with the unloading, but I insisted on going to see the fisherman at once. I wanted to find out what had to be done.

His house was bare, but scrupulously clean. His wife and two small children were gaunt from lack of food, and the woman looked terrified to see Arax and myself. Meriu reassured her while I went to look at the fisherman.

He lay in a bed in an alcove at the back of the large room that was all the ground floor of the house. One arm was wrapped in a rough bandage, but the wound down the side of his face was exposed. The flesh puffed up and his eye was closed. Red streaks ran from the wound across his face and neck. The other eye was open, but I do not think he realized we were there. He was tossing restlessly in a fever.

"Well?" said Meriu, coming up behind.

"It has been neglected. Better if I'd seen it before. But I can help."

I was feeling better, but I knew I would have to rest before I dared tackle the job. Meriu offered to collect herbs for me, and I told her, in as much detail as I could, what I would need and how she could recognize them.

"I'll stay and help prepare the fish," she said. "Then I'll go. I'll have them by midday if all goes well."

"I'll go with you," Arax promised, to my surprise. "And now you," he added to me, "are going back to your room without any argument."

I did not even try to argue. We took our leave and returned through the little town to the palace. I could not pretend not to be tired. By the time we reached the palace gates, I was leaning on Arax's arm. I certainly needed his help up those interminable steps.

It was still not long after sunrise. We met no one but a few early-rising servants who, well trained as always, ignored us.

"Everyone is sleeping off their Festival parties," Arax confided, with a laugh.

"But I thought—the sacrifice . . ."

His laughter died.

"Not at sunrise. Midday. Stay away, Aurion. There's nothing you can do."

He obviously expected me to promise, which I did. But the weight of it was between us as we reached the Fountain Court and my room. Here we met Hithiel, who had just arrived to begin his duties. He greeted us with alarm.

"We spent a rather unusual Festival night," Arax explained. "Bring us some breakfast, would you? Or no—not breakfast." He smiled brilliantly. "Could you make it a very late supper? Hot soup would be good—oh, and bread, and cold meat, and wine, and whatever you can find. Be as quick as you can."

With a bewildered glance at me, Hithiel scurried off.

"I don't really want all that," I said.

"No, but I do." He sat me down on the bed, arranging the pillows behind me, and flung himself into a seat close by. "And you're going to eat something or you're not going down to the town again this afternoon."

I submitted to his autocratic tone. In fact, when Hithiel returned, I found I was glad of the soup. When I had dismissed Hithiel, Arax and I sat sipping it, talking of nothing in particular. I could not find words to discuss the night's ordeal. I could never express my thankfulness to him—not only for giving me my life, but that my stupidity at his party had been forgotten. He was not angry, or not any longer. I was his friend after all.

We had finished the soup and I was thinking longingly of sleep, although reluctant to interrupt this quiet time with Arax. He had gone to investigate the tray of food that Hithiel had left. Smiling faintly, he poured a cup of wine and drank from it. He murmured, "Well, it may be unorthodox, but . . ." and handed the cup to me.

Uncomprehending, I had taken a sip before I remembered and understood.

Wine splashed over the bedcover and the floor as I dropped the cup. Arax bent and retrieved it.

"There's no need to make a mess," he said reprovingly and added, "Don't look so shattered. It's what you wanted, isn't it?"

His eyes were dancing with amusement and triumph, but I had no words. He had completed the ceremony. He was my sworn brother. It was what I wanted, but I found I could not accept it. I felt I had tricked him into it.

"Arax," I managed to say. "Last night—it was a mistake. I'd forgotten . . . I didn't mean it like that. I wanted to give you something, that's all. Arax, I would never . . ."

My voice died away as I saw his face grow cold, the eyes hard. He turned from me, set the cup down deliberately on the table, and said, "You are not Tar-Askan. No one will consider you bound by anything."

He strode toward the door.

"No—Arax, wait! Don't go!"

He stopped on the threshold, no more than an outline against the light. I fought to speak clearly.

"I do want it. More than anything, But I didn't think—ever—you couldn't . . ." I stopped, took a breath, and started again. "Arax, how would I ever have dared?"

For a few interminable seconds he did not move. I was afraid he would leave me and never speak to me as a friend again. Then slowly, he took a few steps back into the room.

"You never thought of brotherhood between us?" he asked quietly.

I shook my head.

"No. Arax, how could I? You're the king's son, and I—I'll never be worthy of you!"

I could not go on looking at him. I hid my face in the pillow and waited for his reply. Nothing came until he touched my shoulder lightly, and I felt him sit on the bed beside me. Only then he spoke.

"Aurion, are you listening?" I nodded. "You're right, I am the king's son. But do you think that makes things any easier? Ever since I was a child and first knew about the bond of brotherhood, I wanted it. I wanted to find someone I could trust like that. I hoped I would, but I always thought I would have to seek him out and ask him, because of who I am. And now look at those—Idric, and Torac, and the rest of them! I would be out of my mind if I trusted my life to any of them for two minutes." His voice grew sharp with disgust. "But they would like it, all of them. To be sworn brother to the king's son—what better way of coming to power? Idric in particular thought I would ask him." He made an inarticulate sound of contempt. "I'd given up, Aurion. I'd put it out of my mind. And then you came along—frightened out of your wits, absolutely helpless, worshiping some crazy god no one has ever heard of. But you never gave up. You never let being frightened stop you from doing what you had to. And you weren't fawning around me like all the others."

He got up and began pacing restlessly around the room. After a moment I got up enough courage to turn and look at him.

"I didn't like it," he continued. "I didn't want to tie myself to some impossible creature from the Two Islands! I tried staying away from you after the leopard hunt, but—well, you know what happened after that."

He stopped his pacing, with his back to me. I wanted very much to see his face. Then he seemed to start talking about something completely different.

"Aurion, do you know that you nearly died of the fever?"

"But—I drank the cordial—"

"You were already worn out. You hadn't the strength to fight it. I told you the fever lasted four days. And Aurion—" Now he turned to face me. There was something desperate in his expression, and I shrank away a little. "Aurion, no one told me. It was three days before I knew. No one thought it mattered to me one way or the other whether you were alive or dead. And it was my own fault." He sighed and passed his hands over his face. "I'd never treated you like a friend. No—" as I tried to protest— "not openly, so anyone would know. I saw we couldn't go on like that. Aurion, once the Festival was over, I was going to ask you. There's a swordsmith down in the town working for me now. And then that stupid party—" He laughed unsteadily. "Aurion, if I'd done it, I would have chosen somewhere a bit less public."

"I'm sorry."

He came and stood over me.

"Well?"

I sighed deeply.

"Arax, I cannot renounce my God, not even for you."

"Have I asked you to? The brotherhood ceremony has nothing to do with the worship of Askar. In that, we can each go our own way. Aurion, you can worship what you like, or nothing at all. I would still trust you with my life."

I hardly dared believe that, after all, everything was coming right. The most I had ever hoped for was that he would accept me as a friend, but not that I would ever be particularly important to him. When he told me about the custom of sworn brotherhood, it had gone out of my mind because it seemed to have nothing to do with me. But he had chosen me. He needed me as much as I needed him. After this, neither of us would ever be alone again.

He must have seen something in my face, for suddenly his mischievous grin was back.

"I can't hang around here all day," he said. "There are those herbs to be found. Can that girl of yours ride?"

"I don't know. I expect so."

He laughed.

"Yes—the horse isn't foaled that would dare defy her! I'll go and see to it. Where shall we meet you?"

"Oh, in the Strangers' Court. I'll need to use my workroom."

"Right." Serious again, he added, "I shall have to attend the sacrifice. I'll see you after that." He stopped and took my hand. "Aurion, in the ceremony we say we have exchanged life and death. We've done that—in the leopard hunt, and the fever, and last night. The ceremony only shows what was there already."

He left me then and went over to the table where he collected a handful of the bread and cold meat that Hithiel had brought. He was halfway to the door before I found words for what I wanted to say.

"Arax, I'll try not to let you down."

He paused, still with that uncharacteristic seriousness.

"You are what you are. You don't have to try."

Then he was gone and I was left alone with my thoughts.

21

Just after midday, Hithiel came from the sacrifice, creeping into my room, clinging to my hand and weeping softly. He told me everything, as if only through words could he unburden himself of the horror he had seen. When he had cried himself out, kneeling exhausted by my bed, I spoke to him a little of God and how he could find love and understanding instead of the cruelty that terrified him.

He looked up at me, uncertain and still afraid.

"But I dare not . . . renounce Askar," he whispered.

"There is no Askar," I replied. "He is nothing but an evil dream. There is only one God, who made all worlds, who loves and protects all His people."

"But I must still attend the temple."

I nodded reluctantly. I could imagine what the priests would do if he failed to give at least outward respect to Askar. Hithiel was never meant to be a martyr.

"God will understand," I promised him.

He sighed deeply and got to his feet.

"I'm sorry, my lord. I'm neglecting my duties." He was attempting to smile. "Do you want to get up?"

I did. I had slept until just before he arrived and I felt refreshed, no longer despairing. However, I had to concentrate firmly on what must be done for the injured fisherman. It would have been too easy to lose myself in wonder and a little fear at the thought of my changed relationship with Arax.

I washed and dressed and Hithiel brought me some food.

"I've work to do," I told him. "Do you want to help?"

He agreed at once, already recovering his usual cheerfulness.

We went down together to the Strangers' Court. Meriu was there, sorting piles of herbs. She had already started to brew the spearwort cordial, which we would need to treat the man's fever. She set Hithiel to watch it. It was obvious to me that she wanted a word with me alone.

"What's this I hear about you and Arax?" she asked abruptly.

By now I was used to the speed with which gossip traveled in the court, but I was taken aback by that.

"We are sworn brothers," I replied.

"Was that wise?"

I had never thought of it as wise or not—only impossible, and then close to miraculous. I did not reply.

"I told you before, Aurion," she went on. "You're too involved with Arax. It's not what you came here to do."

I could see that I would have to tell her everything. Everything from my feeling that I had failed to use the fever cure to bring Tar-Askar to God, my depression, and what had happened at the party that had driven me to try to end my life. If she were critical of my relationship with Arax, then surely she would be even more scathing about the rest of it. To my surprise, by the time I had finished she was smiling.

"Aurion, you are a fool," she said.

"Yes, I know."

"Well, that's something."

She threw back her hair and applied herself to pounding herbs for a moment, and then went on. "So that's how you came to be in my boat last night. Arax was very vague about it. And he did that for you. . . . I can see why you feel as you do."

I shrugged. There was nothing to say.

"Perhaps I'm wrong," she said thoughtfully. "Perhaps God has led the two of you together. Perhaps it's necessary after all."

"I don't know. I can't see how."

"Nor can I, at present. But there might be more sense in it than trying to claim that the healings were a miracle—of all the stupid ideas! You don't really think you could build belief in God on something that wasn't true?"

Her sharp tones were exactly what I wanted to hear. But I

still had to suggest, "If it would have stopped the war . . ."

"It wouldn't. Or if it did, something worse would come. You can't do wrong deliberately, even if the end seems to be good. It doesn't work. As it is . . . well, we still have all that to do."

"I think Hithiel is coming to believe in God."

She smiled, unusually gentle for her.

"Good. And I was talking to the fisherman's wife. . . . It's a beginning, Aurion."

"Only a small one."

"Our Lord had only a small beginning. And on a different world from this. Look what happened to that."

I had to agree, but I still could not forget that war could not be far away.

We worked throughout the afternoon to finish our preparations. Meriu collected everything into a basket and went out with me, sending Hithiel back to his other duties. At the gate of the Strangers' Court, Arax met us.

"What do you want?" Meriu inquired acidly. "Turning up when all the work has been done."

Arax grinned at her amiably.

"I've been talking to my father," he replied. "About you," he added to me.

My apprehension must have shown in my face.

"Well, he had to know," Arax said. "The whole court probably knows by now. In any case, I don't think he was too displeased. You're invited to dine at his table tonight."

I thought that over. Arax fell in beside us and we walked slowly down to the gate and through it into the town. I had not considered before what Largh would think about the bond between Arax and myself. I would have understood if he had been angry.

"He wants you to continue your healing work," Arax informed me. "You can discuss it all tonight."

"What about the priests of Askar?"

"Well, I don't suppose they're pleased. But I told you before, they can't do anything while my father goes on supporting you. He was impressed by the marsh fever cure. So was everyone. Ask for what you want tonight. You'll get it."

The only reply was a disbelieving sniff from Meriu, and we said no more.

To my relief, when we arrived at the fisherman's house, his condition was not much changed. On Meriu's instructions, his wife had everything ready for me. I was able to start at once, working quickly to make use of the light. Arax stood beside me. After a while, absentmindedly, I started giving him things to hold. At the other side of the room I could hear Meriu praying with the fisherman's wife. If Arax was aware of that, he said nothing.

I started by giving the man spearwort cordial, which would attack his fever. Then I cleaned out the wound on his arm, covering it with the salve I had made against infection. Then I bound it tightly. That was fairly easy. But the wound to his face was more difficult, threatening the eye. On the Two Islands I had had proper surgeon's tools, and the knives I had to use here, though sharp, made me feel clumsy. Cautiously I made an incision and watched the infected fluid begin to drain away. Arax made an inarticulate sound of disgust.

"He'll be scarred," he said.

"Yes, but I think I can save the eye."

When the wound was cleaned to my satisfaction, it had to be stitched. I had no thread prepared to do the job, but Meriu had found me some strands of silk that I hoped would be a good substitute. I was conscious of Arax's eyes on me as I worked. Fortunately the man was quiet, too quiet perhaps, but I would worry about that later.

At last I was finished. The wound was clean, stitched, and salved. I went to talk to the man's wife, instructing her what to do and promising to come if she sent for me. Then we said good-bye and left the house. I was surprised to see that the sun was already setting. I felt exhausted, but I remembered that I still had dinner with the king to face.

Meriu left us at the palace gates. Arax stood looking after her thoughtfully.

"She and that woman were praying to your god," he remarked.

"Are you going to do anything about that?" I asked.

He transferred the thoughtful look to me.

"No," he said after a moment. "No, I don't suppose I am."

After another pause he clapped me on the shoulder.

"Come on, what are you waiting for? You still have to make yourself respectable for my father."

At dinner with King Largh that night, the outline was made of the plan that completely reorganized my life in Tar-Askar. He wanted my healing skills, and he was prepared to provide what I needed. Nothing at all was said about the priests of Askar. I was left with a formidable task, but it was one I could do and loved to do.

I was given the permanent use of the Strangers' Court. I never did discover where the palace guests were lodged after that. Meriu was released from her other duties and became my assistant. As soon as she heard that, she moved out of the room she shared with some of the other slaves and went to live in the Strangers' Court. Hithiel also helped, but he refused to give up his other duties as my servant.

My fisherman recovered rapidly, and I had other patients from the town as well as the court. Most of them insisted on paying me, not usually in money, but with fish or fruit or wild fowl trapped in the marshes beyond the point. I passed on a great deal of this to Meriu, who knew which of the townspeople were poor. But there were gifts I was glad to receive and use: a pair of sandals from a leather worker, a bolt of cloth that I had made into a good cloak, a sword belt that I gave to Arax. I could afford to commission a metal worker to make me surgeon's tools. Soon the comparative poverty that had embarrassed me when I first came to Tar-Askar was a thing of the past.

I was released from training with Arax and the others, for I no longer had time for it. Though Arax still insisted on giving me some sword practice from time to time.

"Anything can happen," he said. "I want you able to defend

yourself." But he accepted, as everyone else did, that I would not be a warrior. I would not have to fight in the war against Kerraven. That was a relief, though I reflected I would be more help to Tar-Askar as a healer than I would ever have been as a swordsman, and the thought of the war still weighed on my mind.

I was no closer to preventing it, even though I found as time went on that belief in the true God was beginning to spring up in Tar-Askar. It was known, though never made public, that these matters were talked of in the Strangers' Court. And gradually people began to come there: Hithiel, my fisherman and his family, a slave girl who was Meriu's friend, and others from the town and the court. On some evenings there might be twenty people gathered there to talk and pray. But they were all poor— servants, slaves, ordinary people without power. For all the joy our gatherings brought to me, I could not see how they could affect the war one way or the other. That was proved to me by the fact that Largh, though he must have known, did nothing. If we had been dangerous, we would have been stopped.

In the weeks following the Autumn Festival, I felt torn in two. On the one hand, I still had done nothing to stop the war. On the other, I was busy and happy from morning to night with work that only I could do. I often thought back to the night of the Festival. I had wanted to destroy myself, and that death would have led to Arax dying, and the fisherman, whose wounds would have gone untreated, and now many more whom I was able to help. I understood for the first time that my life was not my own. I would not be so stupid again.

I realized that all I could do was go on with the tasks in hand. There were enough of those. With winter approaching, I had to lay in stores. Meriu and I, and sometimes Arax, went for whole days into the hills collecting herbs. And then there was the work of preserving what we brought back—drying and pounding, making salves and cordials to last until the spring. I also had palace workmen take up some of the paving in the Strangers' Court. I set roots there to begin a garden.

Of course, through all this Arax never let himself be forgotten.

Chapter 22

Even if he were busy somewhere else, he would look into the Strangers' Court and watch the work for a few minutes. Once, obviously enjoying himself, he brought Idric, who had suffered a slight sword cut on the practice ground. Arax was the only one of us not embarrassed as I bound it up.

"If you weren't so clumsy, it wouldn't have happened," he pointed out with a grin.

Idric had the grace to thank me, but I was glad when he was gone.

At other times Arax would insist on dragging us away, asserting that we could not work well if we never had a rest. He was probably right. Winter in Tar-Askar was gentle. There were many days when it was possible to swim and then lie on the beach to eat an impromptu meal. Often Meriu and Hithiel came with us. Meriu, of course, swam as efficiently as she did everything else. Hithiel was a poor swimmer, never having had time to practice. But with three of us to teach him he soon gained confidence—in the water, that is, for he never quite lost his awe of Arax. And so the days lengthened into weeks and there seemed no reason why anything should ever change.

At the turn of the year I began to feel a new urgency. I could measure the time until the Spring Festival, and the thought of it lay like a shadow across my mind. In spring, too, Largh might begin his attack on Kerraven. Few ships would risk the storms of winter, but with the return of the mild weather the way would lie open to Kerraven and the north. Something must be done soon.

One day, with the Festival still some weeks away, I was riding in the hills with Arax and Meriu. We had started early, passed through the valley where long ago we had hunted leopard, and crossed the ridge beyond into a lightly wooded country rising gently before us, veined with small streams that accompanied us with their endless chattering. It was the time of new growth and I was hoping to replenish my stocks of herbs.

We talked as we rode. It was some time before we noticed that a new sound had joined the murmur of water and the noise we ourselves were making. It was a muted roaring, and it seemed to come from above our heads, though we could see nothing beyond the trees. We glanced at each other, puzzled, and then Meriu said, "It sounds like a ship."

"A ship?" Arax's tone was sharp, with an edge of ridicule. At first he did not understand her.

"One of the ships that comes from Centre," she explained. "The ships that fly from world to world. I've seen them, coming to Kerraven."

We urged our horses forward, looking for a clearer space where we could see the sky. I knew, of course, that Ocean was only one of the Six Worlds of which Centre was the chief. And my father had told me of the ships, though I had never seen one. I felt excited at the thought of seeing one now and wondered why it should suddenly appear in the skies above Tar-Askar.

Then we came to the edge of the trees and saw it. It was breaking through the clouds, a slim cylinder of silver, narrowing smoothly to one end. I caught my breath in wonder. Nothing I had heard had prepared me for the actual sight of the ship. Beside me, Arax was frowning at it as if he disapproved. Only Meriu seemed unmoved.

"Something's wrong," she said.

At that I noticed an irregularity in the roaring sound. The cylinder, as it came down, was changing its angle, as if it were out of control.

"Too fast," Meriu murmured.

"But what are they doing here?" Arax asked, his voice angry.

No one answered him. The ship slowed its rate of descent, seemed to hover momentarily over the next ridge, and then disappeared behind it. Meriu let out a long sigh.

"They're down," she said. She looked at me and then at Arax as if expecting something from us. "Well," she said impatiently, when neither of us spoke, "aren't we going to take a look?"

23

Without waiting for a reply, Meriu urged her horse forward, and Arax and I followed. It was about a mile to the next ridge. It was all open country with few trees, but somehow we were in no hurry to reach it. Even Meriu guided her horse at no more than a trot.

"I wonder why they're here," I said. "You've never seen them before, Arax?"

He shook his head. He looked even more displeased.

Still leading us, Meriu turned to reply to me. "I don't suppose they meant to. I expect they were making for Kerraven."

"But that's more than two weeks' sail away," I protested.

"Not if you fly in one of those. I told you, there's something wrong. I've seen them land in Kerraven and they don't land like that. I expect they're damaged."

She was looking quite cheerful and interested. I could not help being more aware of Arax's silence.

"What's the matter?" I asked him.

He looked at me almost as if he were not seeing me.

"What do they want?" he asked after a moment's pause. "Are they friendly, or are they going to attack us? And why do they dare land in Tar-Askar without the king's leave?"

Meriu gave a short laugh, more sarcastic than amused.

"As for asking leave, I don't suppose they had any choice. For the rest, my lord Arax—" the sarcasm was quite evident now—"can you not meet anyone without asking whether they're friend or enemy? They don't attack in Kerraven. They bring trade and news of other worlds. If you ask me, you need to learn in Tar-Askar that you're not the center of the universe."

Arax heard her out without anger. He was scarcely ever angry with Meriu. But all he said was, "Kerraven is our enemy."

We reached the ridge. The ground fell away in a gentle slope before us. There were more trees here and thicker undergrowth. At first we could see nothing, until Meriu pointed out, in the midst of broken branches, a smooth curve of silver reflecting the pale light of the sky.

We moved toward it, and eventually drew close enough to see details. The ship had come down at the bottom of a kind of basin, hollowed in the side of the hill. We had reined in our horses on the lip, looking down. The ship was almost on its side, the nose held up by an outcrop of rocks that thrust through the undergrowth. The smooth surface was crumpled and scarred. A narrow rectangle had opened up in the side. As we watched, two figures climbed out of it, one helping the other. At that distance we could not see their faces, but they were dressed alike, in strange clothes, gray, shiny fabric that covered all their bodies.

The first figure let his companion slide to the ground to lie still. He stood erect, looking around, tension in every line of his body. We were screened by trees. He gave no sign of having seen us. Meriu reached out and touched my arm.

"Aurion, we should go down. That one looks hurt."

I nodded. The slope was too steep for the horses, so we tethered them to branches and went forward on foot. Arax, though he said nothing, set himself at the head of our line, and held his spear poised. We went quietly, but we were not quiet enough. As we stepped out from the trees at the bottom of the bowl, the figure whipped around to face us. She—for to my surprise it was a woman—held something in her hand that gleamed silver. I did not need to be told it was a weapon. She said, "Don't move."

Arax stood still, his spear balanced. For an instant I thought he would throw. Then he lowered it and leaned on it saying aggressively, "No woman in Tar-Askar bears a weapon."

"But I've only just arrived," the woman said. "I'm sorry I haven't had time to learn the custom of the country," she added satirically.

She went on eyeing us warily for another moment and then thrust the silver object into her belt. Meriu stepped forward.

"Forgive us," she said. "Your coming surprised us. Do you need help? My friend here is a healer."

The woman turned to look down at her fallen companion and brushed a hand across her forehead. This was the first gesture that suggested she was not in command of the situation.

"He needs more healing than you could give," she replied.

But the tone in which she spoke was an invitation. I went forward and knelt by the man's side. He was older than the woman, with graying hair. In one place it was dark and sticky with blood that still oozed from a cut on his temple. The position of one arm suggested it was broken. I began to feel his body cautiously, unwilling at first to move him until I knew what his injuries were.

Meanwhile Meriu and the woman were talking together.

"You came from Centre?"

The woman's voice sounded surprised as she replied.

"You know of us, then? No ships have come here before, as far as I can tell."

"But I come from Kerraven."

She told the woman our names and who we were, and that we came from the court of Tar-Askar.

"My name is Hana," the woman informed us in her turn, "and he is Rolf."

She came and knelt beside him, opposite me.

"What do you think?"

"The head wound, and a broken arm. Broken ribs, too, I think." I listened to his breathing; it was shallow, but steady. "I think he should mend, but I can't move him from here."

"Can you send a message to your people?" Meriu asked.

Hana shook her head.

"I don't know. One of the power lines failed and I started to send a distress signal. But I never got off the exact position we came down. I haven't checked the radio since. I'll do it now."

She got up and climbed back through the opening into the ship. I had not really understood what she had said. Meriu explained to my puzzled look.

"They have a . . . a device that speaks from world to world. I don't know how it works, but she can signal to her people and ask them to send help." But after a moment Hana climbed down to us, shaking her head again.

"Smashed," she reported. "I think I can mend it, but it might take days."

"Then we'll have to help you," Meriu said. "Aurion, what do you think?"

She gave me a moment to organize my thoughts. I felt I could do little away from my workroom, and to try to move the man so far might kill him.

"Meriu, could you ride back and bring me what I need?" I asked. "If you hurry, you could be back before nightfall. Arax and I will build a shelter."

Meriu cast a glance at Arax, who still stood motionless at the edge of the clearing, leaning on his spear.

"All right," she said. "What do you need?"

"Linen for bandages," I replied. The meaning of her glance had not escaped me, but I was not prepared to deal with Arax yet. "The salve for wounds, and a flask of the sleeping cordial. He'll be in pain when he wakes. Bring something to eat and drink, and try not to tell anyone what's going on."

Meriu nodded. With a word of farewell she was gone, climbing through the trees to where we had left the horses. I looked up at Hana. She was smiling at me, looking rather shaken. Then suddenly she stopped and touched the cross I was wearing.

"You worship the true God here?" she asked.

"Not in Tar-Askar," I replied. "I don't come from here, either. It's rather complicated. . . ."

"I prayed as we were coming down," she said, disregarding this. "And it looks as if my prayers were answered. Thank you."

She stood up again, looked toward Arax, and then back at me. Then she said, "I'll go and make a start on the radio."

I watched her climb back into the ship. It was obvious that she had noticed Arax's hostile stance and had left me alone to deal with him. Feeling nervous as I had not felt in his presence for weeks, I rose and approached him. He gave me a black look.

"Well?"

"Meriu has gone to bring what I need from my workroom," I told him, though I supposed he had heard what we said. "And we need to build a shelter. Will you help me?"

For answer he lifted his spear and drove its end violently into the ground.

"They are intruders here," he said. His voice held the soft fury that I dreaded. "We should take them back to my father. We should give them to the god."

24

Arax, no!"

The dismay that I felt was not only for the safety of the travelers. It was because they were driving a wedge between us. And most of all it was because I could not bear that Arax should want their death. I stepped forward, grasping his arms. He did not move. The sea-green eyes were hard.

"It is the will of Askar," he said.

He flung me off and strode forward into the clearing, coming to a halt beside the injured man and gazing down at him. I felt as though I had been suddenly transported back in time. Back to my arrival in Tar-Askar, when he had been frightening, unpredictable, and completely out of my reach. The months of brotherhood might never have been.

I was wondering what I could say to him when he swung around on me again.

"Listen, Aurion. Don't be a fool. Look at their ship and the weapon the woman was carrying. We have nothing like that. They could wipe us out, and there would be nothing—nothing—we could do to stop them. Now do you understand?"

"No." I was afraid of him like this, but I still had to try to reach him. "They could do all that, of course. They could have done it already. But they haven't. You heard what Meriu said. They bring trade and news, not war. They would be our friends."

He drew himself up.

"Tar-Askar has no friends, only servants—or enemies."

I stared at him wordlessly. There was gentleness in him, I had found that for myself, but I did not know how to touch it now.

"Arax," I began hesitantly, "my God does not ask for death—"

"Your god is their god, too," he flung back at me. "Of course you protect them—"

"No. I would try to protect anyone, no matter what god they worshiped. And you know it, Arax. I must do what I think is right. When we swore brotherhood—" that was a dangerous topic, and I could not keep my voice steady—"I told you I could not give up my God."

"That's what you're asking me to do." His voice was filled with bitterness. He tossed the spear aside and turned away, his head bowed. I spoke to his back.

"I know, Arax. I'm sorry." When he said nothing, I added, trying to explain, but not sure I was finding the right words, "Arax, it is not only their lives. It's you—I don't want to think of you seeking their death, delighting in sacrifice—"

Still in the same bitter tones, he interrupted.

"I have never delighted in sacrifice. But I have delighted to serve the god."

I went to him at that, and laid my hands on his shoulders.

"We are sworn brothers," he said quietly.

"Yes, Arax."

He straightened up, taking a deep breath, moving away from me, back toward the trees.

"Well? What are you waiting for?" he asked. "I thought you wanted to build a shelter. Or are you going to stand around all day?"

We built the shelter almost in silence. We had made a shelter once before when we had spent a night in the hills. There was not much need to talk. Arax was swift and efficient, cutting small saplings and trimming them with the hunting knife I had given him. We set them up in a tentlike shape around Rolf as he lay, for I still did not dare to move him. Arax lashed the saplings together and I interlaced them with leaves and smaller twigs. He was withdrawn. He was on my side again, but I knew it was the bond with me that held him. He had not changed his feelings about the travelers.

By the time Meriu returned, the shelter was almost finished.

She had brought everything I asked for, and at once I left the work I was doing and went back to Rolf. Arax muttered something inaudible, took his spear, and strode off into the trees. Meriu looked after him, said nothing, and carried on where I had left off, interlacing the shelter wall.

I brought water from the nearby stream, and bathed Rolf's head wound and salved it. I had already set aside two straight sections of wood that Arax had cut, and I used these to set the broken bone in his arm. His internal injuries were beyond me. They would have to wait until his friends came for him. When I had done what I could, I felt I could risk moving him into a more comfortable position. He stirred and moaned as I did so. He opened his eyes, but slid back into unconsciousness without my having to use the sleeping draft. I felt his heartbeat. It and his breathing seemed slightly stronger.

As I sat back I realized that Hana was beside me. She had been for some time.

"How is he?" she asked.

"Better, I think."

I saw she was looking at me in a different way, perhaps with respect.

"You know what you're doing," she said.

"My father taught me. But I can't do everything that should be done. Will your friends come soon?"

She sighed wearily. "The radio still doesn't work. But I'm making progress. Perhaps by tomorrow . . ."

We moved out of the shelter, to which Meriu was now putting the finished touches. The sun was going down. Arax had not returned.

"Where did your friend go?" Hana asked.

"I don't know."

"Will he betray us?"

Her voice was quite level, but she seemed to understand. She must have overheard most of what we said to each other.

"I don't know that either." I did not like that answer, but it was the truth. "I don't think so. But he would not see it as betrayal."

At that moment there was the sound of movement from the edge of the trees, and Arax came into sight. He was carrying something which he flung down at my feet: two rabbits.

"Supper," he announced, a challenge in his voice. "I suppose you realize we'll have to stay here all night?"

"Thank you," Hana said.

Arax ignored her.

"I see no one bothered to get a fire going," he said to me, irritably. "Here, you, girl, go and fetch me some wood."

It was months since he had spoken to Meriu like that. Without waiting for her reaction, he began to collect together the small twigs that were still lying around from the shelter building. Meriu tightened her lips, but she had the good sense to keep quiet. She set off in the direction of the trees. I went with her.

"Can we trust him?" she asked, when we were out of earshot.

"We have to," I replied. And then, feeling disloyal to him even though he could not hear me, I added, "Yes, I trust him."

For if he betrayed the travelers now, he betrayed me, too, for I had helped them. Then the bond of brotherhood that we shared would be nothing but a mockery. I had to trust him. Anything else I could not bear to think about.

When we returned with armfuls of wood, Arax had a small fire burning. Hana was cutting up the rabbits. Meriu had brought bread and cheese, fruit and wine. It would have been a feast, but for my sharp anxiety over Arax. I did not blame him. I knew he was torn in two.

Over the meal, it was Hana who brought up the war with Kerraven. The Kerravene rulers—there was no one king in Kerraven, but a council of lords—had seen Tar-Askar overrunning tiny kingdoms like the Two Islands, and knew that Largh would force all-out war in the end.

"You're the king's son," she said to Arax, leaning forward. Her face was vivid in the light of the fire. "How can we talk to your father? Would he agree to meet the lords of Kerraven?"

Arax looked up at her, his face expressionless.

"When my father sails for Kerraven it will be at the head of his war fleet. And he will meet the Kerravene lords at the end of his spear."

Hana sighed and shrugged, and spoke of something else.

We spent the night there. Meriu and I took turns watching over Rolf. In the early morning he recovered consciousness enough to know what had happened. I judged it was safe to leave him with Hana. Arax, Meriu, and I returned to the court.

"If we stay away much longer, they'll come looking for us," I explained to Hana. "I'll show myself, and then come back later. You may need help with Rolf tonight."

"We may be away by then," she said. "But thank you, all the same. I'd like to see you again before we go."

I did as I had promised. After the midday meal, Meriu and I rode out to the wrecked ship once again. Arax had disappeared, and I did not go looking for him. We took more food in case Hana and Rolf had to stay there longer. I had half expected to find them gone already. When we dismounted at the top of the slope I could see no one, but when we came to the clearing, Hana was emerging from the ship. She waved to us, smiling.

"I mended the radio this morning," she told us. "Help is on its way."

"How is Rolf?" I asked.

"Better, I think. He was awake for quite a while earlier, but he was in some pain, so I gave him your sleeping draft. He's quiet, now."

I went into the shelter, checked Rolf's condition, and renewed the dressing on his head wound. As Hana had said, he was quiet. If help were coming, there was nothing more to worry about. Outside I could hear Hana and Meriu talking to each other. From the few words I caught, Meriu was telling her about our work in the Strangers' Court and the group that met there to talk about our God, and about our hopes of stopping the war.

When I came out again, Hana was grave-faced.

"I admire you," she said. "But look, it's impossible. No one can ask any more of you. I've been thinking—we'll be leaving soon, maybe within the hour. Why don't you come with us, to Kerraven?"

I stared at her. For a few seconds I could not take in what that would mean, and then it rushed in on me like the breaking of a storm. I could leave Tar-Askar. In Kerraven I would be among people I could understand, people who worshiped my God. I would no longer be an exile. I might even see my father again. Or if that was not possible, I could at least write to him and receive letters in return.

Then I looked away. It was not possible. If I left Tar-Askar, the only chance of stopping the war would leave with me. And there was the work I was doing. And overwhelmingly, there was Arax. If I never went back to the court, he would know where I had gone. I could imagine his sense of loss and betrayal. Slowly I shook my head.

"I can't. Thank you, but I can't."

"I can't, either."

That was Meriu. Instantly I turned to her.

"But Meriu, it's your home!"

She shook her head.

"This is my home now. This is where I'm needed."

Hana was smiling at us, her eyes bright.

"I thought you might say that," she told us.

Before either of us could say more, there was a crashing sound behind us. Arax burst out of the trees. He was breathless, white-faced, frightening me because I had never seen him like this. He dashed up to me and grabbed my arm.

"Aurion—" he gasped. "Get out—get away—"

Suddenly Hana cried out in alarm. I followed her eyes. All around us, on the edge of the bowl, dark against the sky, were horsemen, carrying spears.

"Aurion," Arax cried, "I swear I didn't—"

The horsemen dismounted and began to move toward us, down through the trees.

Hana's hand went to the weapon she wore, but she did not draw it.

"I can't," she said.

Beside her, Meriu stood motionless. Arax was still gripping my arm.

"Aurion," he said urgently, "I didn't lead them here. Do you believe me?"

I nodded slowly.

"Yes. Yes, Arax, I believe you."

I caught the ghost of his old swift grin as he turned to face the spearmen. Now they were hidden by the trees. Only slight movement and sound told us they were advancing. Within minutes they would reach our clearing, and there was no escape. Then a yard or two from the shelter I thought I could discern a shimmering in the air that swiftly grew until it became an iridescent gray, the size and shape of a doorway. Hana gave a cry—a sound of joy and relief.

"It's the ship!"

I did not understand.

"It's the way into the ship," she explained impatiently, already stooping into the shelter. "Our friends have come. It's a kind of door. You can walk through it—go on, quickly."

None of us moved. In spite of the danger, I was lost in wonder to think that a step through the curtain could take us into a ship so far above us that we could not see it. Then Hana reappeared, supporting Rolf.

"You must come with us now!" she exclaimed.

I felt Arax's hand on my arm tighten, and then he released

me. Meriu shook her head.

"No, we can't."

"But they'll kill you!"

"Meriu's right," I said. "We belong here. Whatever happens, we'll have to face it." As Hana still hesitated, I added, "But you must go. Please—don't worry about us."

To my relief, she began moving slowly toward the glimmering curtain.

"You're mad—quite mad," she said, but she was smiling warmly.

Then she and Rolf disappeared into the opening. Behind us there was a hoarse shout, and a flung spear whistled past my head. It fell harmlessly as the shimmer faded out. We were alone. All around us the spearmen were emerging from the forest.

"Well," Arax murmured, "at least this should be interesting."

We were taken back to the court and to the presence of the king, in the small room where I had been summoned to attend him before. For some time he sat with his chin on his hand, looking us over in silence. His eyes were dark and unreadable. Finally he spoke.

"Take the girl away. She is no more than a woman and a slave, and had no choice in what she did. Go back to your duties, girl."

Meriu opened her mouth, but I flashed her a look. To my relief she closed it again, turned, and left submissively. There was no point in her sharing our punishment. When she was out of the room I almost felt that I could relax.

King Largh turned his gaze back to us and then waved the guards out of his presence before he spoke again.

"You may wish to know how you were discovered," he said. His voice was too quiet. "You were not the only ones to see the ship come down. One of my huntsmen was in those hills. He saw you, and those who came in the ship. But he at least knew his duty and reported it to me. At first I did nothing. I waited to see if you would come to me. But a night and part of a day went by, and you did not come."

He paused, looking past us into some unseen distance.

"My own son." Now there was the lash of anger in his voice. "My own son is a traitor to his country and to his god. Well?"

Arax was standing rigid, his mouth tight.

"My lord," he began, "it was not my intention to be a traitor. But I—"

"I persuaded him, my lord," I interrupted. "At first he wanted to tell you. I begged him not to, and he gave in to me—because we are sworn brothers."

"Yes." The king shifted, and the impenetrable gaze was fixed on me. "And why did you do so?"

"I am a healer, my lord, and the man was injured. And I knew of no harm that they had done to me, or to Tar-Askar." I took a breath. I felt I could not save myself, so there was no point in hiding anything. "And the sacrifice to Askar is an abomination. I would not give them up to it."

I heard Arax's sharp intake of breath, but the king ignored it.

"Indeed," he said. "Your god, of course, demands no such sacrifice?"

"No, my lord."

"It was in his service, then, that you helped and protected these people?"

"Yes, my lord."

He gave his attention back to his son.

"And you helped. Or at least, you did not hinder. Are you also a servant of this strange god?"

Arax flushed.

"No, my lord. I serve Askar."

"Very imperfectly, it seems. You have deprived him of his rightful sacrifice."

"I didn't mean—my lord, I did it to protect Aurion!"

The king said nothing more, seeming to withdraw into a deep concentration that neither of us dared to break. I wondered what he was waiting for. I could not even feel afraid. I thought that the only possible ending would be death.

At last the king let out a long sigh.

"And now what am I to do?" he asked. "My son. My only son, who will be king after me. And the hostage who is under my protection and who keeps the Two Islands safe in my power. What am I supposed to do with you?"

Neither of us spoke. It was obvious he did not expect an answer. Finally he waved a hand dismissing us.

"Very well. You may go."

We were both too shocked to move. At last Arax managed to say, "My lord?"

"Go." I felt that his voice was under tight control. A lesser man might have shouted. "The punishment for blasphemy is death, but how can I put either of you to death? Go—get out of my sight!"

We went, still too shocked to take leave properly. We did not speak until we were out in the open on the terrace outside the king's apartments. Arax took a breath like a swimmer coming up for air and sank down on a stone seat.

"That was not pleasant," he stated.

"I'm sorry, Arax. It was my fault."

He shook his head at me, half smiling.

"You couldn't help it. You are what you are."

"At least it's over."

His smile faded, and was replaced by a frown. He looked uncharacteristically thoughtful.

"Maybe—"

I felt a stab of fear, more than I had felt in the presence of the king.

"What do you mean?"

"Oh, use your head, Aurion!" At least it was more familiar to have him exasperated with me. "Think what we can be charged with—blasphemy, treason. . . . And he lets us go. Just like that."

"But he said—"

"And you believed him? Aurion, hostages have been put to death before now. So have kings' sons, if the cause seemed good. We have a long tradition in Tar-Askar of solving problems in the . . . most direct way. No, Aurion, I don't like it."

Hearing him say that, I did not like it either. And though life went on in the normal way, I was conscious all the while of an underlying thread of uneasiness.

As time went on, this uneasiness was replaced, or joined by another. The Spring Festival was upon us. Once again the sacrifice to Askar would be chosen. This time I had no excuse not to stand in the courtyard with the others. And there was Hithiel, now totally committed to the true God, and others who came to speak to us in the Strangers' Court, all opposed to Askar and the sacrifice. And all of us helpless to do anything about it.

The day of the Spring Festival came with a clear, pale light. A sky almost without color arched over the temple courtyard. I stood in the crowd with Arax and Hithiel. I saw now up close the same scene that I had watched from a distance on the morning of the Autumn Festival. King Largh sat enthroned in his golden robes, a remote figure, though I was standing not far from him. The scarlet-clad priests made their preparations, while the trumpeters waited for the rising of the sun. This time the smoke from the coals in the copper bowl rose steadily in a thin column into the still air.

I felt I ought to say something to Arax or to Hithiel, who stood quietly beside me. His courage was no longer in question. But I could think of nothing to say. And indeed, the whole assembly was silent, as expectancy grew and laid hold of us like a great hand. In my mind I formed a prayer—not words, but a mute offering of all of us, king, priests, and people alike, into the protection of God.

I do not know why my gaze should have fallen on the king in particular, but as it did I saw with a sudden chill that he was looking at me. His face was expressionless, his eyes hooded and unreadable. But all the time those eyes were fixed firmly upon me. And I knew. In an instant of time I knew what he had done and I understood why. Arax had seen it too. I heard a sound from him and felt his hand grip my shoulder. Then the edge of the sun glittered its way above the palace buildings. The trumpets arced up and spoke their harsh note. The priest before the copper bowl raised his arms and cried out a single name.

My name. It was no surprise to me. For a moment, everything was very clear, as I turned to Arax and saw in his face the knowledge that we shared. I could hear the stir around us and

Chapter 25

Hithiel breaking into distraught sobs. Then the sounds blurred and seemed to break over me like the waves of the sea. Arax's face was suddenly tiny and distant. I was aware of nothing but the small, triumphant smile on the face of the king.

125

26

I do not think I ever lost consciousness, but for some time my mind refused to work. Even now, looking back, there is a gap of several hours in my memory. I can recall what happened in the courtyard, and then nothing, until the shock ebbed away and I found myself alone in the temple.

Though I had never been there before, I understood where I was, for Hithiel had told me every detail of the sacrifice. At first I lay passive while my senses seeped slowly back. Then I began to think rationally again. I knew I had lain there for a long time with dim light and silence all around me. I tried to catch the peace that was slipping away from me, but it was no use. I half sat up and looked around.

I lay on a marble slab about the size and height of a bed. It was covered with a white linen cloth, but the cold struck up from it and chilled me to shivering. I was naked except for another linen sheet. They had stripped me of everything—even the cross my father had given me.

Four lamps were burning, one at each corner of the bed. But apart from this, the room was in darkness. The corners were draped with shadow. There were no windows. At the far end I discerned the darker shape of a single door. I knew that I lay in the innermost room of the temple of Askar, and I would not leave it again until they came to take me to my death.

Apart from the bed and the lamps, the room was empty. I could hear nothing, and there was nothing to tell me how long I had lain insensible. The sacrifice would take place, I knew, at midday on the day following the Festival. But how close or how far off that was, I did not know.

I sat erect, pulling the sheet around me as if it could shut out the cold. As I moved, I noticed on the floor beside the bed a tray with a jug and a cup set on it. The sight of it made me realize how thirsty I was. I reached out to it, but stopped as I remembered what Hithiel had told me. The wine or water or whatever was in the jug would be heavily drugged so that the victim might shut out the terror of approaching death.

Even as I stopped there was part of me that wanted it. I knew that I should face the sacrifice in my right mind without the help of a drug. But I was dreadfully afraid that at the last I would break down. Arax would be there, watching me. I did not want him to remember me a coward. I drew back from the jug, but it remained there, a silent temptation.

I tried to think. I knew that for me there was no hope. I was deep inside the temple, guarded not only by men, but also by the fear and reverence of Askar. No one who might want to save me could reach me now. The king had won.

Fighting against fear, I recalled with difficulty the knowledge that had sprung upon me with such clarity when I met his eyes in the courtyard. He would not put his own son to death. But he would not accept as his son's sworn brother, a hostage from a different people, worshiping a different God, who had influenced his son to betray his loyalty to his own people and his own god. Yet he could not put to death a hostage who was supposed to be under his protection.

Or only in one way. For the sacrifice was chosen by Askar himself, or so the king wished all his people to believe. No one could accuse the king now of having any part of my death. He was clever. Even now, here in the temple, I had to admit that.

Waves of terror were washing over me, and thinking coherently became more difficult moment by moment. I remembered Meriu and Hithiel and wondered how they would fare when I was gone. And I wondered about the war. It was inevitable now. The little protest I had made seemed laughably feeble.

I do not know how long I sat like this, fighting panic, fighting the temptation of the drug, trying to force my thoughts toward God instead of the ordeal to come. The lamps burned steadily. The flames were bright in their intricate copper housing. I wondered if they would burn until I was taken out. I felt that if they failed and I was left in darkness, that last thread of my sanity would snap.

And yet I did not know how close to panic I was until the stillness was broken by a soft movement. It came from the shadows, down toward the dark opening of the door. I tensed and choked back a scream. Were they coming? Was it time? I had left it too late for the drug. I wanted to run and hide. I could see myself being dragged out of a corner, shrieking out into the sunlight and the ranks of watching eyes. I did not move, staring toward the door as I saw the shadows shift and gather together into a single figure that stepped forward into the pool of light. It was Arax.

I could not move. When I tried to speak his name, it came out on a sob of terror. He strode forward. His footsteps were soft but purposeful. He was the great, lithe cat again, and the hunting light was in his eyes.

"Here," he said, as he came to my side and thrust at me a bundle he was carrying. "Put these on—quickly."

He was, of course, not there. I was asleep, or in the madness of fear. I had drunk the drugged wine without knowing it and he was the dream of disordered senses. The bundle slid to the floor and scattered, for I could make no move to take it. Arax breathed out my name on a sigh of exasperation and stooped to collect the fallen garments.

"Pull yourself together," he ordered. His voice had an urgent undertone. "Here—we haven't got all night. Oh, let me do it."

He pulled the tunic over my head as if he were dressing a very small child. Suddenly, at the touch, I knew that he was there. He was real. The paralysis dropped away from me. I would have clung to him, but he held me off and made me finish putting on the tunic, deftly fastening it because my hands were shaking too much.

"How did you get in?" I asked.

He grinned—that mischievous grin I had thought I would never see again.

"That girl of yours gave me some sleeping draft from your workroom, and I mixed it in some wine and brought it for the guards. Everyone gets drunk on Festival night, even a temple guard, with a bit of luck."

"But Arax—"

He passed the tunic belt around my waist and began to buckle it. The tunic was wool, warm after the chill of the marble and linen, but I could not stop shivering.

"You'll have to go tonight," Arax went on. "Meriu has arranged all of that. She's waiting for—"

"Arax!"

I clutched at him and this time I made him stop and listen to me.

"Arax, the guards will know it was you who drugged their wine. If I'm gone, they'll punish you, kill you in my place, perhaps . . ."

He nodded, his eyes dancing.

"Certainly, if I were here. But I won't be. I'm coming with you."

I started back away from him.

"No! Oh, Arax, no. You can't. One day you'll be king. You can't give that up. I won't let you."

"You can't stop me."

"I can if I stay here. You can't make me come with you. I could cry out—rouse the whole temple. . . ."

My voice died away. He was looking at me with an odd, twisted smile.

"You would do that?" he asked.

I nodded. The smile broadened and became pure enjoyment.

"But you can't, Aurion," he explained. "It's all done. As you said, the guards will know who drugged their wine. Even if you were here in the morning, I've still committed blasphemy enough to send me to the sacrifice with you. And really, what would be the point of that?" He stooped to the floor. "Here—sandals. Can you manage?"

While I fumbled with the straps, he sat on the slab beside me and went on reflectively.

"I saw my father's face this morning. He knew it would be your name the priest cried out. He knew! If he truly believed in Askar he would not dare! And if Askar truly exists, and has the power we believe, he would have struck him dead for his impiety!"

His calm was dropping away from him, and although he still kept his voice soft, the note of anguish grew plain to hear.

"I was proud to stand in the courtyard before the god and offer my life along with my people. But now—I'm no more than a fool. There is no Askar. I was risking nothing. Would the king allow the sacrifice of his only son? I wonder how many of them knew?"

He turned away from me, his breathing harsh and ragged. I reached out to him, wanting to offer comfort, and suddenly he was standing over me, gripping my shoulders painfully.

"Aurion, did you think I would let them kill you?"

I had no answer, between wonder and shame, for I had not believed that he would have thrown everything away to save my life. I had not really trusted him. I felt tears start, and at that he released me with a little shaken laugh.

"You see, I've found that I can't really do without you—you or your crazy God." Before I had time to think what that might mean, he went on swiftly, "So if you're quite ready, we'd better go. Unless you would rather stay chatting for the rest of the night until the priests come in the morning."

I was on my feet before he had finished speaking. I could understand well enough that if I gave way now, his sacrifice would have been for nothing. He flung my cloak across my shoulders and pulled something from the pouch at his belt and held it out to me.

"The priests would not let this enter the temple," he said. "I salvaged it. I believe it means something to you?"

It was my father's cross.

27

Arax led me through the door at the end of the room and along a short passage into a much larger hall, lit by shafts of moonlight that struck through windows high in the walls. A dark mass loomed in front of us. As we skirted it, I realized it was a statue of Askar. It was larger than life-size, a robed figure seated on a carved throne. I hesitated, looked up, and almost betrayed myself by crying out. Above the brocade-clad shoulders, the moonlight glanced silver on the gaping head of a fish.

Arax grabbed my arm and pulled me on. At the next door were two guards, slumped on the floor and snoring. A scatter of wine cups and fruit from a bowl lay on the floor beside them.

"How much did you give them?" I asked in a whisper.

"A flask of the stuff between two jars. Meriu thought that would be enough."

I had paused, looking down at the guards.

"Well, they should wake eventually."

He urged me on again.

"Aurion, no one but you would think of such a thing at a time like this!"

Another passage, and then the main doors of the temple. They were closed. Arax pulled on the bronze handle until the door swung back enough to let us through. He closed it again behind us. Two other guards lay in disorder on the outside. We were standing on the steps where King Largh had presided over the assembly that morning. Now the courtyard was deserted. We made our way around it close to the wall, clinging to the shadows.

"No guards on the archway," Arax murmured. "Just as well. Let's hope the street is quiet."

He peered out of the gate and then beckoned me through. No one was about. As we hurried on down toward the palace gates, we could hear the noise of celebration. I remembered how I had fled from Arax on the night of the Autumn Festival. Now he brought me to the same gate I had used then, leading out on to the stretch of the beach. Moonlight glittered on the water and a breeze whispered over it. A boat was pulled up on to the sand and three figures stood near it: Meriu, Hithiel, and a fisherman whose face was seamed with scars.

Hithiel flung himself at me and clung to me, sobbing.

"Take me with you, my lord! Please take me with you!"

I tried to comfort him. Across his head, Meriu commented, "Well, you took your time."

She could not give her voice quite its usual tart abrasiveness. I smiled at her, but I could say nothing, realizing how much I was going to miss her brisk demeanor and her caustic tongue. I wondered if I would ever see her again. And Hithiel—I could not expose him to the risks of a journey in a small boat when I did not even know where we were going. But he would have Meriu to look after him.

Arax touched my arm.

"Come on," he said. "Before someone takes it into their head to have a moonlight swim. . . ."

We crossed the sand to the boat.

"I've provisioned it," Meriu said. "If you're careful, you should be able to last until you get where you're going."

"And where's that?" I asked.

She looked me up and down pityingly.

"Kerraven, of course," she replied. "Where else?"

"Kerraven!" Arax exclaimed, looking surprised and displeased. To him, Kerraven was still the enemy.

"Oh, Arax, don't argue!" Meriu snapped. "Just go!"

He opened his mouth to protest again, and she went on hurriedly.

"I've got a plan. No—" she overrode another attempt to

interrupt—"there hasn't been time to work it out properly, and there isn't time to tell you now. Go to Kerraven, make yourselves known to the council of ruling lords, and wait to hear from me."

Arax looked at me and shrugged helplessly. I could already see that Meriu was right. Apart from tiny kingdoms like the Two Islands; Kerraven was the only place we could reach in a small boat, the only place where we could expect to be safe. And yet if Kerraven gave shelter to two blasphemous fugitives from the power of Askar, would that not make the war inevitable after all?

Meriu waited a few seconds, but neither Arax nor I had anything more to say.

"Then if that's settled," she continued tartly, "perhaps you wouldn't mind getting a move on? I assume you know how to navigate this thing?"

Arax's bewilderment had to dissolve into his familiar grin.

"After a fashion," he assured her.

We turned to the boat again and started to push it down to the water. After a moment I stopped and caught at Meriu's hands.

"If we're going to Kerraven, won't you come with us?"

She shook her head.

"We've been through all this before. I'm needed here—even more after you're gone. I've got to carry on your work in the Strangers' Court—all your work. Besides, don't forget my plan."

There was a flash of wicked amusement in her eyes. In the midst of danger, she could enjoy tantalizing us. I understood that, and I understood her reasons for staying. But it was hard to say good-bye.

Now Arax was calling my name. The boat was bobbing on the water. He and the fisherman were holding on to the side. I hugged Meriu and Hithiel, who was still struggling with tears. I splashed through the shallows to the boat and pulled myself over the side. Arax, already aboard, pulled up the sail and I felt the wind take it. The boat suddenly came alive. I scrambled for the tiller. When I looked back, several yards of water separated us from the beach. My fisherman, knee-deep in water, raised a hand to us. Further away on the beach, Meriu and Hithiel stood together. I waved, and watched until their figures dwindled to dots.

"Dreaming?" Arax muttered, and added after a pause, "what was all that about a plan?"

"I don't know."

He frowned up at the taut sail, and then I saw him slowly relax.

"Never underestimate that girl," he said thoughtfully.

We were already approaching the mouth of the bay. I concentrated on what I was doing, holding the boat in mid-channel as Arax trimmed the sail to take full advantage of the wind that would drive us north to Kerraven. Part of me felt it was an adventure. I was going out into the unknown, and I was with Arax. But the rest of my mind was confused and afraid as I wondered if I were facing the failure of all I had set out to do.

to us. Farther away on the beach, Meriu and Hiruld stood together. I waved, and so did Hiruld. But Meriu neglected.

A high tower in a castle on the coast of Kerraven. I sat in the window seat and looked out over the sea. The sun shone. I could almost imagine that I was still in Tar-Askar, but the gray walls that fell away beneath me were nothing like the flowered terraces of Largh's palace. And the wind from the sea had a keen edge, even in summer, that they never felt in the south.

I will say little of our voyage. God was good to us and we had fair winds. We saw few other travelers, friendly or not. We landed on small islands, mostly uninhabited, for fresh water and to supplement Meriu's provisions by catching and cooking fish. It was a month almost to the day when we landed on the southern coast of Kerraven.

Durac, the lord of that domain, was himself a member of the ruling council, and he made us welcome. We told him our story. The threat of war was no news to him. The council was already making plans to counter a Tar-Askan attack. Durac treated us well, but he brushed aside what we had to say about Meriu and her plan. Of course, he had never met Meriu. What he did was to send word of our coming to the other councillors. We were still waiting for a reply. And we were still waiting for a move from Tar-Askar.

We had been two weeks in Kerraven when word finally came. Arax had gone riding, but I had been told that a merchant ship was about to leave for the Two Islands. I had stayed behind to write a letter to my father. That was done and I was idly watching the sunlight on the water when I heard hurrying footsteps on the stairs outside. The door burst open. Arax stood there, his eyes lit, his body taut with excitement.

"A Tar-Askan ship!" he exclaimed.

I got to my feet.

"A warship?" I asked.

"Yes, but flying a flag of truce." Breathless, he flung himself into a seat on the other side of the room. "Coming into harbor now," he went on. "I wanted to go down, but my lord Durac told me to wait."

I turned and looked out the window again, but a headland hid the harbor mouth and I could see nothing. After his first elation, Arax was giving way to impatience.

"It must mean something," he said. "Do they want us handed back? Or are they declaring war? Or both?"

"At least it's one ship," I replied, "not the whole war fleet. They've come to talk, not fight."

Arax nodded. He could not stay in his chair, but began to pace the room restlessly. He had borne two weeks of waiting without complaint, but the next two hours tried his patience—and mine—to the limit.

The sun had sunk low over the sea before a light tap came on the door. Arax stopped in his pacing. The door opened and the Kerravene servant who stood there announced, "An envoy from Tar-Askar!"

I had time for no more than a second's surprise that the Tar-Askan envoy should come to seek us out as I had to face an even greater shock when the envoy swept into the room and confronted us. It was Meriu. Arax and I stared at her, then at each other, and Arax collapsed into helpless laughter.

Meriu gave him a pitying look and came forward to embrace me formally.

"My lord Aurion."

"My lady."

It was what she looked like, dressed in fine linen, with her hair curled and interlaced with ribbons and a gleam of gold at her throat. But the snapping eyes were familiar, and the acid in her voice as she said, "You might ask me to sit down. I've been three weeks at sea, and all on your account."

I motioned her to a seat. The sound of the door closing made me turn to see Hithiel, looking shyly delighted.

"I don't believe it," Arax said. "I shall wake up in a minute."

Meriu sniffed.

"Rubbish! Instead of standing there gaping like idiots, you should be asking me how I came here."

Before we could ask her anything, we were interrupted by the return of the Kerravene servant with a tray of wine, fruit, and sweet pastries. But I was able to dismiss him as Hithiel insisted on attending us. When the four of us were alone again, Arax continued.

"Lady, you have our profound admiration." His voice changed. "Now would you mind telling us what this is all about?"

Meriu sipped from the cup Hithiel had handed to her.

"I have to go back to the night you left, or rather, the morning after when the king discovered you were gone."

"He didn't punish you?" I asked.

"No. He questioned both of us and the fisherman who provided the boat. But there was no evidence to connect me with the drug in the guards' wine. And two desperate characters like yourselves, guilty of blasphemy and treason, wouldn't stick at stealing a boat. Largh isn't unjust, whatever else he may be."

"And then?" Arax asked.

"And then I let things cool down. There was no hurry. I had my plan worked out, and I wanted Largh to have time to realize exactly what it meant to have lost his only son and the heir to his kingdom." She gave Arax a smile of catlike satisfaction. "You didn't think he would write you off quite so easily?"

Arax was silent, totally absorbed in what Meriu was telling us.

"If you had stayed," she went on, "the priests would have forced his hand. But given time, I knew he would think of a way around it. After what he did to Aurion, you surely don't think he believes in Askar any more than I do? So after a week, I went to see him."

"Just like that?"

Meriu shrugged.

"I told him that you had gone to Kerraven."

"And he believed you?"

"As I said that night, where else could you have gone? He believed me. And so I pointed out a few other things to him—such as the fact that you had given yourself up to the Kerravene lords as a hostage against the war that he was planning."

Arax was on his feet.

"You did what?"

Meriu looked up at him unmoved.

"Sit down. Stop fussing. You should know by now that here in Kerraven they would never use you as a hostage. You would be safe, even if your father launched his attack. But he didn't know that."

"What did he say?"

Meriu's lips tightened.

"He wasn't pleased. In fact, for a few minutes I thought he might forget himself and have my head. But that would have meant admitting that a woman had driven him into a corner—and what Tar-Askan warrior could admit that?"

She shook her head, amused, brushing aside her danger and her courage.

"After that he dismissed me. Two days later I heard that he had made an announcement to the priests, that Askar had appeared to him in a dream and commanded the forgiveness and the recall of his son."

Arax stared.

"You're not telling me the priests believed that?"

"What else could they do? Accuse the king himself of blasphemy? They'd be braver men than I take them for, if they did that."

"So what happened next?" I asked.

"Largh sent for me. He said that since I seemed to know all about it, and was Kerravene born, I had better go and help negotiate your return. To tell you the truth, by then I was getting on with him rather well."

Arax nodded. "He likes a good fighter."

"So I set sail," Meriu told us. She flicked a hand dismissively. "There's a Tar-Askan lord or two with me, of course. And I asked for Hithiel because I knew he wanted to see you again. The ship travels faster than your boat, but it took us a few days to find out where you were. And here we are."

Arax let out a long breath.

"And here you are," he repeated. "And I'm a hostage."

"For the time being."

"But I can't—" he began to protest, and stopped.

"Yes, you can." Meriu was as downright as ever. "Do you really want a war to the glory of Askar, after all that's happened?"

He paused, and then slowly shook his head.

"There is no Askar," he said. "My father knows that, but he uses the fear of Askar to strengthen his rule. And now I know it. And when I am king, I will show my people a better way."

He turned to me, smiling.

"There'll be a treaty, Aurion. Peace, not war, just as you always wanted. You can go home."

I had never thought of that. It was Arax's fate I had been concerned with, not my own. Now I remembered the low hills of the Two Islands, and the way the wind took my sails as I tacked around the point and saw the white walls of my father's house among the trees. I felt a sharper pang of homesickness than I had ever experienced in Tar-Askar.

Then I realized that there was a sense in which Tar-Askar was my home too. And all my life I would be homesick for the hills and forests and my work in the Strangers' Court—for Hithiel's gentle loyalty, for Meriu's friendship, and for Arax, who had been ready to throw away a kingdom for my sake. He was my brother and one day he would be a noble king. He would forge the Tar-Askans into a noble people, in the service of the true God.

Now Arax was looking at me intently.

"Didn't you hear what I said, Aurion? You can go home."

I smiled at him and held out a hand.

"Well," I said, "there's time enough to think about that."

Storm Wind

"I'm not going!"

The war had always been distant—nothing but newscast reports or stories from men home on leave. But now that the war is getting closer, Randal's mother is sending him to Altir—which is supposed to be safer—but he does not want to go. Determined that Altir will be boring and he'll detest his cousin, Randal quickly discovers that his expectations are anything but reality. He and his cousin Veryan soon find themselves far more involved in the fallout of the war than they ever dreamed they would be.

As the two journey through the city filled with destruction, Randal is faced with more decisions than he's faced in his life, one of which is the biggest decision he'll ever make—whether or not to take God seriously.

Visit a time when the Six Worlds were young, before their people lost contact with Earth, before the Black Years began, before it was dangerous to believe.

Cherith Baldry is involved with literature, especially children's books, in all aspects of her life. She is a teacher and school librarian and has two children of her own. She and her family live in England where she enjoys writing, reading, and gardening.

Chariot Books™
A Division of Cook Communications

Cradoc's Quest

"Life must be more than this."

Legend tells of a Book and a belief that the ancestors from Earth once held. It's an almost-forgotten belief—until now. For reasons unknown to him, Cradoc—a young farmhand who longs for something more from life—is chosen to bring that belief back to the people of the Six Worlds.

Cradoc discovers a copy of the Book, thought to have been destroyed during the Black Years. It contains truths that could cause the greatest upheaval in the history of the Six Worlds. Cradoc must get the Book to a printer so its truths may be widely read, but there are many who will try to stop him—and destroy the Book—along the way.

The people of the Six Worlds long ago lost contact with Earth and the belief of its people. Journey through the Saga of the Six Worlds and discover, as they do, that what's gone may not always be for good.

Cherith Baldry is involved with literature, especially children's books, in all aspects of her life. She is a teacher and school librarian and has two children of her own. She and her family live in England where she enjoyes writing, reading, and gardening.

Chariot Books™
A Division of Cook Communications

✦ PARENTS ✦

Are you looking for fun ways to bring the Bible to life in the lives of your children?

Chariot Family Publishing has hundreds of books, toys, games, and videos that help teach your children the Bible and apply it to their everyday lives.

Look for these educational, inspirational, and fun products at your local Christian bookstore.